THE PHANTOM FIREFIGHTER

FIRST RESPONDER
BOOK ONE

J.W. JARVIS

BIG DEE
BOOKS

JOIN MY VIP READER CLUB

J.W. Jarvis' VIP Reader Club members get free books, access to discounts, and other unique items to accompany the books.

Members are always the first to hear about J.W. Jarvis' new books and publications.

See the back of the book for details on how to sign up.

The Phantom Firefighter
by
J.W. Jarvis

Copyright © 2023 by J.W. Jarvis
Published by Big Dee Books

~

For all of the brave First Responders
who run towards danger while others flee

~

CHAPTER
ONE

A HIDDEN PLACE

N oah was in a bad situation. He had to keep running forward swiftly, or he would have slipped off the narrow, windy, old bamboo bridge. Sometimes, when the body has momentum, any sudden stop or change in direction will undoubtedly result in a loss of balance. Falling into a greenish-yellow swamp was not only going to tempt the nearby reptiles but would also be embarrassing. Noah's partner was already on the other side waiting for him. As he approached the end of the bridge, a giant Pteranodon with a rider wearing a cowboy hat swooped into him from the right and snatched up his golden devil toad achievement. As Noah flew into the murky abyss, he heard the sound of wet, long, and probably horrendously stinky farts coming from his dog lying next to him on the hardwood floor.

"Ugh! It took me forever to find that toad! Hold on, Tanner," said Noah as he quickly found his phone under his dog to stop it from farting. "Hello?"

"Morning Kiddo, what are you doing?"

"Just playing *Triassic Traveler* with my online friend. Where are you?"

"I am working, and you should be too; I left a list of chores on the kitchen table."

Noah sighed. "Okay... okay, why are you working on a Saturday?"

"I need to catch up, and you want to eat, don't you?"

"But you're always working; can't we have some fun?"

"Sure, after your chores are done. Call me when they are; I need to go." Then, his dad ended the call.

Noah's dad was always working, especially after the divorce. His mom had left them once the pandemic subsided. The government and businesses had made stay-at-home orders to slow the virus spread. Being forced to live, work, and go to school in the same home every day caused a strain on his mom and dad's relationship. Noah never saw his mom, except on major holidays, because she moved closer to her work, two states away. During the pandemic, she got a new job but could work remotely. After the pandemic, the company forced them to come into the office three days a week. Their breakup forced Noah and his dad to move to a less expensive town about two months ago. It sucked. His dad had to work harder and longer hours so they could afford to live on their own.

Why was his mom so selfish? Noah always pondered.

Worse, Noah had no brothers or sisters to play with or share chores with. He'd struggled to find friends after their move. Noah had left behind a group of buddies in their old town and was not the most outgoing person. He felt alone when his dad worked, except for Mumu, their Alaskan malamute.

"Move Mumu, you are in my way," Noah was trying to get up from the couch in their living room. Mumu got up and bowed toward Noah with a wagging tail. Mumu wanted to play, so he grabbed one of his toys and tossed it toward Noah. "Not now, boy; I need to get something to eat and do yucky chores." Mumu's wagging tail stopped, and he crouched on the floor, putting his sulking head between his front paws. Noah petted Mumu softly on his head. "Sorry buddy, give me an hour."

Mumu was a large dog at about 75 pounds. He was grey and white with piercing blue eyes. Malamutes tended to shed a lot, especially during certain times of the year, which was why Mumu was not allowed to go upstairs in the carpeted area of the house. The downstairs was all tile and wood floors. Noah's dad had a robotic vacuum that was especially good at cleaning dog hair. Noah remembered when the vacuum was broken, and he had to sweep the entire house downstairs. When he was through, the amount of fur in his pile looked like the son of Mumu!

Noah threw two frosty pastries into the toaster oven, poured himself a glass of orange juice, and sat at the kitchen table. Noah began cleaning the boogers from his crusty, still sleepy eyes. He had gone straight to his game console after waking up.

"Ugh!" he cried.

The chore list in the notebook was longer than a page.

Am I supposed to be a slave to my parent? he thought.

The doorbell rang just as Noah was about to bite into his second pastry. Since he was home alone a lot, his dad had a video doorbell that he could access from his mobile phone. His dad wanted him to always check his phone before answering the door. He pulled up the phone app and saw it was his neighbor, Tommy. Tommy was three years younger than Noah, so he immediately looked up to him and wanted to hang out, especially on the weekend. Noah didn't mind having someone in the neighborhood, but Tommy had different interests, and some of them were too childish for Noah, like playing with plastic army action figures.

Noah opened the front door. "Hey Tommy, what's going on?"

"Want to play cornhole, Noah? I just set it up on my front lawn."

"Jeez… sorry Tommy, my dad has a list of chores for me to do that is a mile long."

"Want some help?"

"Umm, no thanks; I just want to knock them out before my dad gets home from work. Maybe, tomorrow?" Noah felt bad as Tommy's face soured, but he knew if Tommy helped, it would take longer because Noah would have to tell him exactly how to do everything.

About two hours later, Noah's phone started farting again. He got nervous when he saw the caller ID because he had only finished six of the ten chores on the list.

"Almost done Dad," Noah said as he accepted the call.

"Well, at least you're making progress. Why don't we go downtown?"

"For?" Noah dragged the word out slowly.

"Does Belly Busters sound good?"

"Sure… and maybe the sports store?"

"I'll think about it. Be ready in 15 minutes; I will pick you up."

They had moved to a smaller town called Primrose Beach. Downtown was only about a 10-minute drive from their home, so they went there often. Downtown consisted of one main street lined with different establishments. The street included restaurants, clothing, and antique shops. There was also a smaller sports store on the corner that Noah and his dad often visited, especially during baseball season. Because the weather was extra frigid, the downtown was less busy than usual, so parking was easy.

They walked into Belly Busters and immediately got hungry from the yummy smells in the air. If you weren't hungry before entering, you were as soon as you walked in. Belly Busters was one of Noah and his dad's favorite restaurants because it served what his dad called *comfort foods*.

"Where would you like to sit, gents?" asked the owner with a welcoming smile.

"How about the rock and roll corner?" asked Noah.

"Ahh, I knew it, and I was saving that table just for you two," the owner said with a wink.

The corner table had a little box where you could select different songs to play while you dined. The table also had a half-circle booth with very comfy leather seats. They quickly ordered two bowls of their favorite soup,

New England clam chowder, and a couple strawberry lemonades.

While waiting for their food, Noah asked his dad, "Can we go to the sports store after dinner? My baseball cleats are super tight."

"Sure, but I thought I just got you those," said his dad.

"Last year, Dad." Noah rolled his eyes.

When their food came, they lifted their spoons and ceremoniously clanked them together to celebrate their good menu choice.

Noah said, "Cheers, Big Ears!"

His dad responded, "Same goes, Big Nose!"

They didn't say this as insults but because it was funny and rhymed. Noah's dad had told Noah a while ago that he learned that saying from visiting a pub in Australia. Noah giggled every time they did it.

They headed toward the exit when they finished dinner and paid the bill. They thanked the restaurant owner because their bellies were satisfied. When they turned left towards the sports store, the wind picked up with a crisp chill. They immediately regretted leaving the comfort of the warm cozy restaurant. As they approached the store, everything looked dark inside, and a sign hung inside the door. It said the owners were on vacation this week and would return Monday to re-open the store.

"Aww, they suck," said Noah.

"Hey, that's not nice to say, Noah."

"Why?"

"So, they don't deserve a vacation once in a while for their hard work?"

"We don't take vacations, but we work hard."

His dad sighed, "We will someday, Son; times are tough now since your mom left."

"What's that?" Noah caught a glimpse of a store across the street.

"What? Where?"

"Over there, Dad," he answered, pointing with his finger eagerly.

"I don't remember that being there. Is it new?"

"No idea, but I can see lights on inside; let's check it out."

As they approached the store, it was hard to make out the sign because green ivy had grown over the top of the door. There was so much ivy that it hid the store entrance. No wonder they'd never seen it before. The front of the store had a grey and black brick surface with a dark, wooden door. The windows were stained glass, like at a church, so the light shone through, but it remained hard to see inside the store. Walking closer, they could make out a handmade wooden sign above the door, reading *Barton's Books*. They pushed down on the door handle and walked in as curiosity overcame them.

Immediately, they noticed how small the store was, but it didn't matter because there were books from the floor to the ceiling everywhere. It seemed like it would take a lifetime to read them all. Yet the store appeared abandoned since they didn't see any other customers, an owner, or even a caretaker.

"Can I help you?" came a scratchy, weak voice as a person appeared from the dark corner of the room.

Noah and his dad turned around and saw an older woman standing behind a counter. The woman was probably in her seventies. She had long white hair, almost silver, and golden reading glasses hanging from her nose. She wore a purple and black robe as if she were about to hop into bed or take a nap. They walked over to her.

"Sure!" said Noah as he immediately focused on the enormous wart on the old woman's nose.

Not only was it keeping her glasses from falling off, but it also had two black hairs sticking out of it. He tried not to stare at it as he asked.

"Do you have a children's section?"

"Let me show you, child."

It seemed to take her five minutes to move from behind the counter. She raised her arm slowly and pointed to a wall behind Noah near the opposite corner of the store.

"They are all here on these five shelves. As you can see, we have nothing on the higher shelves that children can't reach. Those shelves are for adult children, like your dad."

"I beg your pardon," said Noah's dad with a confused look.

"Ooh, I didn't mean to offend. Aren't we all children in God's eyes?" the old woman asked.

Noah's dad stared at her for a long second, looked away, and then replied, "I guess."

The books all seemed to have unique-looking covers as they approached the wall. Some were leather covers; others had buckram cloth-type covers. They came in a wide array of colors. There were no paperback books, only hard-bound books, which was strange for a children's section. Thicknesses varied from approximately one to four inches, and the titles of the books only appeared on their spines. Noah's gaze was directed toward a red book just above his eye level with the title, *The Fearless Firefighter*. He paged through it, and decided that it looked interesting enough, especially with its detailed illustrations. He couldn't find a price on the cover; however, none of the books had price tags.

"How much for this one?" Noah inquired.

"The books are not for sale, child."

With a bewildered look, Noah asked, "Then... can I check it out, like at a library?"

"We are not a library, child," she said.

Noah looked at his dad and gave him his biggest puppy eyes to plead for help.

"Listen, lady, we don't understand. So, we can't read your books?" his dad asked.

"Sure, you can. Just take them but please return them when you are done," she said.

"Okay, do you need some information from us so you can keep track of your book borrowers?" his dad asked.

"Nonsense!" she exclaimed. "You look like nice people. Enjoy, enjoy! But now I must ask you to leave as I am getting tired and closing soon." She motioned toward the door hurriedly.

Noah politely thanked her as he headed for the door.

While on their way home, Noah's dad commented how strange it was for this store to let people take books, but Noah assured him he would return it when finished. Noah was excited to read it and told his dad how cool it was to have found this hidden place in their little town. Noah now had another reason to go downtown and didn't need to spend his allowance!

TWO

SPIT TURNS PAGES

I t was late when Noah and his dad got home, so Noah went upstairs to shower and get in his pajamas. His nightstand had other books and toys, so he quickly tossed them into the closet. His dad wouldn't notice the messy closet if the door were closed. He placed *The Fearless Firefighter* book on his nightstand. Since his mom left, his dad worked all the time. They rarely had one-on-one time together, except for sharing the occasional meal. Weekdays were much worse than weekends. Today was extra special, with dinner together and a story to read. Noah had been reading a lot lately since he had not yet made friends at his new school. He would much rather go on real adventures with friends, but a good book would take him there for now.

He finished showering and went downstairs to the kitchen to prepare one of his favorite story time snacks.

"Dad, where are the cocoa packets?" Noah yelled to his dad upstairs.

His mom had always been good about putting them out on the counter before story time when they'd all lived together.

"They're in the cabinet above the microwave," his dad yelled.

"Okay, what flavor do you want?"

"Caramel!"

Noah couldn't reach the cabinet, so he grabbed a step stool from the side of the refrigerator. He grabbed one mint and one caramel packet. The kitchen had a machine on the counter that made coffee, tea, and, most importantly, any hot chocolate flavor. All one had to do was drop the flavor packet into the machine, put a cup under the machine, and in 45 seconds, a steaming hot drink was ready. Noah just had to add marshmallows. Noah loved this machine and vowed to his dad that he would one day have a machine like this when he had his own home.

After the cocoa was finished, they went to Noah's

bedroom and got comfy in his bed. It was also a tradition on the weekends to read books together. They did this for years, starting when Noah was two years old. It was much easier when Noah was younger to read together almost every night, but homework and early-to-bed school nights got in the way as he got older.

They picked up their cups and clinked them together before taking a sip, "Cheers, Big Ears! Same goes, Big Nose!" they said in unison.

At this point, Noah remembered something he had learned on the internet.

"Do you know why people started clinking their cups together before drinking?"

"Because they were celebrating something?"

"No, but I'll give you one more guess."

"They wanted to see whose cup or glass broke first?"

"Come on, Dad, think Middle Ages here."

"I give up, Son!"

"They did it because they figured a little of each person's drink would spill into each other's cup when they were banged together. If one of them were trying to poison the other, then they both would die!"

His dad laughed and said, "Well, I'm glad you didn't poison me this time."

Noah picked up the book from the nightstand and opened it to the first page. The book opened very stiffly as if it had rarely been opened. This was strange, given they learned in the store that these books were borrowed, not bought. Noah would typically read a chapter out loud, and then he would hand over the book to his dad to read the next chapter. It depended on how long each chapter was. Taking turns reading made story time more fun for them.

The prologue chronicled the life of a firefighter named Zach and his actions after high school to become a firefighter. Those steps included medical training, fitness training, and volunteering to build experience. One of the reasons Zach desired to become a firefighter was because he hadn't cared much for school. Instead, he liked doing physical work and helping people.

That's just like me! thought Noah.

Zach joined a firehouse and took its training, a six-month program. The chapter explained that Zach had been a firefighter for almost five years, including a promotion to lieutenant. A lieutenant had more responsibilities, including assisting with new firefighter training and firehouse operations and acting as captain when the actual one was absent. Zach liked when that happened and aspired to be a full captain himself soon.

Noah arrived at the start of Chapter 1, titled "How I accidentally became a captain. "

He wanted to keep going, even though it was his dad's turn.

"I know it's your turn Dad, but can I keep reading?"

"Sure, are you enjoying the book? I was wondering what made you choose it."

Noah thought momentarily and said, "I've always wondered what I want to be when I grow up. I love the color red, think fires are fascinating, and would love to be able to help people like a superhero."

"Well, that's commendable, but remember, it is also very dangerous. Why do you think fires are fascinating?"

"The way something burns is so random, it seems. When you watch logs burn in the fireplace, you never know which will burn the fastest or where it will break; it's like a dancing flame with no official choreography."

"You are so smart, Noah. That's very insightful."

"Not to mention, the sooner I get a job, the less you'll have to work, and we could spend more time together."

Noah's dad's eyes grew watery as he grabbed a sip of his hot chocolate to try and hide it. Chapter 1 was about how Zach was out on a fire call to a 10-story apartment building. He, four other firefighters, and the fire captain arrived on the scene to see flames billowing out of the fourth story. Noah started to turn to the next page but couldn't quite grab it with his finger. His dad explained a neat trick to help.

"When it's hard to turn a page, just lick your finger and slide it at the corner of the page to pick it up."

"Gross, Dad! That will put my spit in the book!" Noah commented immediately.

They both laughed at the thought, but Noah conceded. Something bizarre occurred as he turned the page with his spit-covered finger.

CHAPTER
THREE

A STRANGE FEELING

Noah and his dad heard a word whispered to them that they couldn't understand, "Enciddugo!"

At that moment, Noah's dad could see the burning building, hear the fire burning, and smell the heavy smoke. He looked down where his hands should be, but they weren't there. Scared bystanders, large emergency vehicles, and busy firefighters surrounded him. He felt strangely attached to one of the firefighters, like he was floating above him. What had happened to his body? Was he dreaming this after reading about it in his son's new book?

After hearing the same, strange word whispered to him, Noah felt a tingly sensation on his skin. It was like the feeling you get with goosebumps but way more intense. Like his dad, he could now see a large building partially on fire and many people and firefighters running near him.

What was happening?

He also felt the weight of something heavy on his body and head. He looked down and saw that he wore gloves and boots, which he was not wearing before story time with his dad.

Just then, Noah heard someone call "Zach!" and his instinct made him look up to see the firefighter that said it was staring right at him.

"Zach, snap out of it! The captain needs help in the building!" firefighter Ray exclaimed.

"What do you mean, my name is..." Noah caught his words realizing that he had never seen this person before in his life, and for some reason, this guy thought he was a guy named Zach.

"We need to get inside right away. The captain went

in to check for remaining building occupants, and something happened."

"How do you know?" Noah asked while still trying to internally process his transformation into Zach, the firefighter.

"You didn't hear on your helmet headset? Captain said part of the ceiling came down, and he needs muscle," replied Ray.

"Got it. Do we need to bring anything?"

"Jeez, Zach, why do you think they call me 'Rookie Ray?' You're the experienced one here."

"Alright Ray, follow me!" Noah said, thankful that he knew the name of the guy he was going into a burning building with.

Noah motioned to Ray to follow him toward one of the entrances. Noah headed toward the building with a strange mix of both nervous and confident feelings. His firefighter uniform was much heavier than he'd expected, but it gave him some comfort to know it would help protect him from dangers. He became anxious since he was entering a burning building without knowing anything about being a firefighter. Yet, his body was somehow mysteriously trained on what to do next.

Noah's dad heard the whole conversation and wondered why firefighter Zach had hesitated at first in an emergency. He also wondered why when Zach moved, his presence followed him. He didn't want to go into the burning building, but he had no choice; he had no legs to move him in the opposite direction. It was no different than the view you got when playing a third-person shooter game on a video game console. The problem was Noah's dad had no controller to control his player, i.e. Zach.

"Zach, wait!" Noah's dad yelled, but the firefighter didn't turn around. He tried one more time screaming at the top of his phantom lungs. "Can you see me?" Again, there was no response, so he flipped his apparition self backward and saw Ray running toward him. "Ray, your mom's belt size is equator!"

Nothing. Ray didn't react at all. Normally, guys laugh hard at good momma jokes.

As they entered the building, Ray saw the elevator was lit up and working,

"This will be faster; the stairs could be blocked," Ray told Zach.

"...and if the power goes out, we'll be stuck. Trapped firefighters are no good to anyone." Noah was suddenly impressed at how intelligent his reply was; maybe he did know something about firefighting.

They headed toward the stairs and put on their oxygen masks as they headed to the fourth floor. The trip up the stairs was more challenging than expected, as the weight of the uniform and the oxygen tank on Noah's back felt even heavier with each step. As they approached the door to that floor, Noah could feel the air temperature around him increase. It felt similar to stepping into a sauna but much worse and smokier. The door would not open as the heat of the fire had warped the building structure, essentially causing the metal door to seal to its frame.

"Use the axe on that door, Ray!" Noah shouted.

Ray lunged with all his weight, sending the axe into the middle of the door. It made a six-inch dent.

"Not like that; remember your training," Noah said, that firefighting knowledge of Zach's was working through him somehow.

"Sorry Boss, the hinges and the handle... got it."

"Quickly... we don't know how much time we have here." Noah was losing patience.

Ray made four swings of the axe, three on the left side hinges and one near the door handle; instantly, the door moved a few inches. Noah instinctively rammed it with his shoulder, and it fell to the ground inside.

Wow I'm strong! he thought in awe.

They proceeded over the threshold and lifted the door

to place it over the opening. Fires need oxygen to grow. Keeping doors open to other areas of the building increased the chances of more oxygen reaching the fire, extending and ultimately prolonging it.

Noah could hear some chatter on the built-in speaker inside his firefighter helmet, "Hurry, we're in a bad position on the southwest corner of the building!"

The captain and his partner were trying to describe where they were on the fourth floor. They were stuck somewhere. One of the most important things about being a firefighter was never entering a building alone. Going into dangerous situations in pairs allowed each firefighter to have a backup in case something went wrong. Something had gone wrong while the captain was searching for trapped occupants and figuring out how to keep the fire isolated. As soon as Ray and Noah entered an area in the corner of the building, it was clear what had happened to the captain.

The room was sweltering, but luckily, there was no visible fire. The fire was in the middle of the floor, but there was only one wall between their location and the primary fire. The fire had extended to the ceiling and caused one of the ceiling structural beams to crack in half. Unfortunately, the shaft broke right as the captain reached the last occupant of the building. It fell on his back and pinned his right leg to the floor. Luckily, his oxygen tank had broken most of the beam's weight instead of snapping the captain's back.

"I know you don't like me, Zach, but you didn't have to make me wait in a burning building." It was good to see the captain's humor was still intact.

"Well, I was just worried about Jimmy here, honestly."

Jimmy was the captain's partner that went into the building with him.

Wait, how did I know his name? Noah quickly thought. *I must have all of Zach's firefighting knowledge now.*

"If you are done pining over Jimmy, do you mind getting the ceiling off my leg?" urged the captain.

"If we can lift it a little, can you move your leg out?" asked Noah.

"Unfortunately, not; when I tried to move it, it felt like 1000 knives were stabbing my leg all at once."

Noah surveyed the room. Next to the captain and Jimmy was a young woman who looked scared. She was the person the captain went into the building to save in the first place. The oxygen tank that broke the beam's fall on the captain hissed like a rattlesnake as the pressurized gas escaped from its gaping hole. The ceiling and room next door were crackling loudly as the fire made its way through the wood framing of the building. The smoke was getting thicker, so everyone took turns inhaling from Jimmy's still functional oxygen mask.

The group didn't have much time.

Ray motioned to Jimmy and Noah to grab the end of the beam closest to the captain's leg. Even with three strong firefighters, it barely moved. But as it did, the captain gasped and screamed, "Arghh... son of a gun!"

The wood beam had numbed his feeling in the leg, but as soon as the weight was removed, the blood rushed back into his leg, and his nerve endings exploded with agony. They were able to move the beam enough to free the captain's leg, and they dropped it on the floor next to him.

"We need to get out of here now, everyone!" Noah commanded. "Jimmy, can you take her? Ray, help me get the captain up slowly; I'll carry him down."

Noah's dad observed the room and felt helpless. He could not help, but he'd wanted to. At the same time, he was probably as scared as the young woman because it felt so real. He shuddered every time the fire in the room next door blew out another glass window from the building. The smell of smoke was disgusting, but it wasn't like he was breathing; he had no body. He felt anchored to Zach as the firefighter moved around. He wondered why he was even there if his presence served no purpose. This was just a dream, and he hoped to wake soon. He had no clue the third-person view of Zach was actually that of his own son, now inhabiting the firefighter's body.

For Noah, it was too real to feel like a dream. He knew he was a trained firefighter but couldn't understand how. He could only focus on getting to safety outside of the building. Instinctively, Noah knew the proper method to carry someone. It was something taught at the firefighter academy. It involved carrying the victim on his shoulders by draping the victim's stomach over the shoulders like a scarf and holding the victim's dangling arm and leg with the hands.

Noah was careful only to hold the captain's good leg.

He yelled over the sound of the ferocious fire, "Everyone, follow Ray!"

"Lady, take my hand." Jimmy motioned to the woman.

"Are we going to die? I can't see anything, and my lungs are burning," she shouted with a shudder.

"I got you; that's what we're here for," Jimmy answered.

At that moment, part of the wall beside them gave way and fell right into the very spot they had just moved from. Half a second later, the fire burst into the room, craving more space to grow, and instantly ignited the leaking gas from the damaged oxygen tank. The tank exploded, sending metal shrapnel everywhere but specifically at Jimmy, who was the last to leave the room. It tore right through his fire jacket and into both of his arms. He shrieked in pain but was more concerned with protecting the woman.

"I'm okay. Are you hit?" Jimmy asked as he visibly struggled.

She was in a state of shock from the explosion but eventually nodded.

"Keep moving, everyone!" Noah's voice could still be heard through the black smoke.

They reached the door to the stairs that had been axed down by Noah and Ray earlier. Ray moved it aside, and they headed downstairs. Every flight of stairs they passed brought them cleaner air and more visibility. The walls started to flash red and yellow random patterns, making everyone realize it was the emergency vehicles' lights peering through the glass door at the front of the building.

It was a welcome sight.

FOUR

RESCUE REWARD

As they approached the exit, the team on the ground already had a wheeled stretcher, also called a gurney, ready to place the captain on at the door. The gurney was taken straight to the ambulance to help stabilize the captain's leg. Everyone else moved toward the fire truck to get oxygen. Their lungs had taken in smoke, and it caused them to cough and wheeze, like when someone has asthma. Inhaling fresh oxygen helped to open the airway passages in the body so smoke-inhalation victims could breathe more freely.

"Take long, deep breaths," said one of the para-medics. "It'll help you get relief faster."

"Yes, it will help open your airway passages," Noah said as he gazed at the rescued woman. "Jimmy, that was a pretty loud explosion up there; you were the closest to it."

"Yeah, we should all play the lottery because our timing was nearly perfect before that wall collapsed. Unfortunately, I did get hit on my arms."

He turned around, and the back of his arms appeared to have metal scales sticking out of them like he was part dragon.

"Ouch, you need to get that looked at. It could have hit a major blood artery in your arm. Buddy, can you take a look at this?" Noah yelled over to the paramedic attending to the woman.

Noah's dad looked back at the building. He saw that the rest of the firefighters were fighting the fire from an extended ladder on the firetruck. They were spraying a powerful stream of water through the broken windows. The sound of the water accompanied glass windows cracking and breaking under the heat of the fire. The fire was much smaller than when they first arrived on the scene. Noah's dad heard one of the firefighters yell back to Zach that they had the fire 80% contained.

One hundred percent containment didn't mean the fire was gone; instead, the firefighters had kept it from spreading more. Noah's dad thought he would give it one more try to see if anyone could hear him.

"Zach, Jimmy, Ray... anyone, can you hear me?" Noah's dad got flustered and raised his voice to the highest volume possible. "Don't be scared; I'm not a spooky ghost. I just want to know if you can hear me. If you can, raise your right arm."

No one did.

Everyone was busy getting treated for their wounds or talking with the rest of the team over their radios.

Noah's dad thought to himself, *Now I know this must be a dream because I remember not being able to do all the things I usually can when I'm dreaming.*

The captain and Jimmy went to the hospital with the paramedics in the ambulance. Noah, well more accurately Noah-as-Zach, was now the highest-ranking firefighter on the scene. The rest of the department depended on his guidance now.

"Alright, Captain, what's our next move?" One of the firefighters asked Noah.

"Uhh… the captain just left for the hospital. Are you blind?"

"…which makes you acting captain now on this scene, Tonto!"

"Well, my first order is that you will be cleaning the fire truck tomorrow." Noah wasn't happy with the other firefighter's tone or the fact he called him a "fool" in Spanish. The firefighter immediately regretted what he'd said. Noah turned around, took a deep breath, and whispered, "You can do this; make your dad proud."

At that moment, while it felt real, he still wondered when he would wake from this dream. His dreams had never been this detailed.

Noah clicked the talk button on his radio and asked all firefighters, except those on the ladder fighting the fire, to gather near the tiller truck. A tiller truck was a firefighting vehicle with a specialized turntable ladder attached to a semi-trailer truck.

Noah's body host, Zach, had years of training and experience that kicked in as he spoke.

"Alright, the building is vacant now; we must suppress that fire from more than just the outside because it is spreading to the floor's interior. We need to get a hose to the standpipe valve in the stairwell."

The standpipes run vertically through the building in the emergency stairwells. The team had already connected the hydrant on the street to the main valve for these standpipes, which was on the outside wall of the building.

"I'll take Jack and get the hose hooked up ASAP," said Ray.

"Did anyone check with the building owner to ensure there are no gas lines on the fourth floor?" replied Noah.

"Already did," said Jack, "and we turned off the gas to the first floor, just in case."

"Nice work, guys; let's get to work and make our sauna in the gym jealous of this building's fourth floor," Noah joked.

When fires were put out with water, the water is converted to steam, which could still be very hot at a balmy 200+ degrees Fahrenheit. While steam could be a good thing, it still could easily burn a firefighter if one were caught in the direction of it.

It took another two hours to extinguish the fire completely. The fire investigators, who also worked for the fire department, were called to the building to figure out how the fire started and who or what was responsible.

The paramedics cleared Noah and the rest of the department to return to the firehouse. On the way back, Noah reflected on what had happened. He couldn't believe he was now a lieutenant in the firefighter company. Everything that had happened was thrilling, scary, and exhausting simultaneously.

He suddenly became anxious.

If he was here, where was his dad? Was his dad okay? Was his dad one of the other firefighters? But wait, this was just a dream, right? His dad was probably concerned watching his body convulsing in bed while Noah was dreaming.

His head was spinning, and he wasn't sure if it was because of everything that had happened or the amount of smoke he'd inhaled. He also wondered if he was stuck forever in Zach's body. It was satisfying to have helped save the captain's and the woman's lives, but he already had a life as a kid with minimal responsibilities. He didn't want the duties of an adult just yet.

While Noah's dad was not physically there, his presence was. He could see the firefighter, Zach, thinking hard about what happened and felt his concern for some strange reason. He wished he could say something to make Zach feel better, but no one could hear or see him. Noah's dad started to worry as well.

Was he trapped as a spirit following these firefighters? Why did he have this connection with the firefighter Zach?

He felt close to him but had never seen him before today.

Where was his son? Was his son back at their home? thought Noah's dad.

On the ride back to the firehouse, Noah's dad decided to try to talk to Zach again. Everyone was exhausted from the long evening, so it was tranquil inside the truck cabin. The fire scene was chaotic and loud from the glass breaking, jets of water, sirens, and the crackling fire. It made sense no one could hear him yelling. Noah's dad figured it might be better to get closer to Zach's right ear and whisper loudly.

"Zach, can you hear me?"

Noah turned to Jack, sitting on his right side, and looked at him funny. Jack was staring down at his phone, texting his wife about the firefight. Noah turned his head back.

"Great job tonight; you're a good leader!" Noah's dad whispered.

"Thanks Jack," Noah replied.

Jack turned to Noah, "Huh, thanks for what?"

"Oh... I appreciate the compliment," answered Noah.

"Dude... I didn't say anything, but you're right; I should thank you for stepping in for the captain tonight. You did well and thanks for bringing us home safe."

Noah turned his head back and felt very confused. Noah's dad, on the other hand, was beaming with joy.

He heard me, he heard me, he thought.

He desperately wanted to start talking to the other firefighters but didn't want to freak everyone out. It was bad enough that Zach probably felt he needed to get his head checked for injuries. For the next 20 minutes, the firefighters checked in with their loved ones on the way back to the fire station. Something about being in extreme danger made them want to reconnect with their families.

Noah was amazed at its size when they arrived at the firehouse around 8 p.m. The garage was easily able to hold multiple fire engines and emergency vehicles. The garage was meticulously clean, and so were the fire trucks. It was impressive how many controls and equipment were on the fire trucks. They were bright red with chrome plating and knobs all over them. Noah started touching the knobs and flipping the switches off and on like a kid in a candy store. The weird thing was he strangely knew how to operate everything on the truck. From reading the book's prologue, he remembered that Zach had been a firefighter for five years. Now his knowledge of firefighting equipment made sense. They all made their way to the kitchen, as it was late, and no one had dinner yet.

"I'm starving; anybody want a pizza?" Ray asked.

"I sure do," as Jimmy walked behind everyone into the kitchen smiling.

"You're back from the hospital… so, I guess the cuts weren't severe."

"Well, it took a while for them to pull the ten pieces out of my jacket and arm. They had to cut up my jacket so they could see how far the pieces went in before removing them. It kept me from bleeding out."

"Yikes!" said Ray. "I see they gave you a souvenir."

Jimmy shook a glass jar, and it made a clinking noise as the shrapnel recovered from his body collided inside. "Yep, this one is going in the trophy case!"

It wasn't really a trophy case with gold and silver awards, but all the firefighters used it in the house to put various knick-knacks from their firefighting adventures. Some were related to people they'd helped, like thank you gifts and cards, while others were reminders of their close calls with death, like Jimmy's shrapnel.

On the kitchen wall was a calendar. It had the schedule for every firefighter in the company. Noah saw his name with a work shift ending at 10 p.m. that day. It was a 24-hour shift followed by two days off. Noah was surprised firefighters were on-call that long, but at least they could rest for a couple days.

At almost 10 p.m., he got a phone call. The caller ID showed "Captain."

"How are you feeling, Captain?" Noah asked.

The captain responded, "Well, thanks to you, I'm alive, but unfortunately, my leg is broken in eleven different places."

"Sorry to hear that, Cap. Are you still at the hospital? Is there anything I can do?"

"Well, since you mentioned it, yes."

He stated that his return to service would be months, not weeks. It might possibly take over a year. He then went into how he had planned to retire soon and that maybe this latest fire was the push he needed. To Noah's surprise, the captain explained how he felt Zach was the most qualified firefighter to replace him. Becoming fire captain was the next step up from fire lieutenant, so this was a natural move. Noah excitedly thanked the captain for the opportunity, and they ended the call.

Noah realized his shift was over as the clock showed 10 p.m., and suddenly, the tingly skin sensation he had felt earlier that day came over him. After his eyes blinked, his vision was blurry, but as it cleared, it revealed his dad sleeping beside him.

CHAPTER
FIVE

ALMOST PERFECT DAY

Noah saw his dad had fallen asleep next to him and was relieved that his whole experience had been a dream. He couldn't wait to tell him about it in the morning. The weird thing was, why did he feel so exhausted if he had been sleeping? He also thought it was strange how he could remember almost every detail about his dream when usually he never did. He got off the bed slowly, not to wake his dad, and went to the bathroom to brush his teeth. They were drinking sugary hot chocolate during story time, and he didn't want his teeth to rot like his mom had always said would happen if he forgot. The firefighter book had fallen under the bed when they dozed off, and he could have sworn he saw it glowing as he returned from the bathroom.

Confused, he reached under the bed to grab it. It looked perfectly normal as he placed it back on his night-stand. He thought, *Great, now I'm seeing things,* as he pulled the covers back over him.

The next day, Noah and his dad went about their usual Sunday schedule with a homemade breakfast of pancakes and sausage. Most people would only put their maple syrup over their pancakes but not Noah. He liked to put the maple syrup on the plate first, so the pancakes at the bottom got as much syrup as the ones on top.

"So... how did you like the book, Son?"

"Umm, eh wha soo sore wheel..."

"What? Hey what did I say about talking with your mouth full?"

Noah swallowed his pancakes, "Sorry, Dad, it was so surreal! When I fell asleep, I dreamed the whole thing about Zach saving the captain from the burning building. It was terrifying because it felt like I was actually there. I could feel the heat, and breathing was difficult with the thick smoke."

"Wow, I felt the same way, only I couldn't help; it was

like I had no body but most of the body senses, sight, hearing, and smell. Zach definitely earned that promotion after carrying the captain down four flights of stairs. We must have finished the chapter because we remember the same story. Honestly, Son, now I'm baffled."

"I've been wondering, do you think this is fiction or a real-life experience someone wrote about?" asked Noah as he took one last bite of his juicy sausage link. He couldn't finish all his links, so he dropped his last two in Mumu's bowl.

"Hard to tell at this point. Maybe we'll figure it out after we read the rest of the book," said his dad. "Many books have experiences that could happen in real life too."

Today was much nicer outside than yesterday. The temperature was in the high 50s, but the sun was shining, so it felt much warmer. They decided to get some base-ball-catching practice in while it was warm. Noah played the center fielder on his baseball team, so catching was crucial. The best way to keep the opposing team from scoring runs was to keep them off the bases. Catching fly balls was all that mattered. Depending on the hit, Noah could be running and catching simultaneously, as he had a wide area to cover. Mumu helped with practice too. When

Noah missed a throw from his dad, Mumu would retrieve the ball and bring it to one of them. Their home was on a cul-de-sac with three other homes. Fewer cars were on the road, making it a perfect place to play catch.

"I forgot to tell you at breakfast, but your mom called last night. She came into town."

Noah's eyes lit up, and he said excitedly, "Can we see her?"

"Of course, she thought it would be nice to meet at the beach since it'll be a nice day today. We're meeting her in about an hour."

"Can we bring Mumu? He misses her too!"

His dad smiled. "Absolutely!"

Noah's dad owned a four-door silver pickup truck. They packed snacks in a cooler and beach folding chairs and put them in the truck bed.

Noah said, "Up, Mumu!"

His dog quickly jumped into the back of the truck. Mumu was only about two years old, and Noah wondered how many years he could keep jumping that high before he would have to help him.

Primrose Beach was near the downtown area they went to on Saturday. The actual sandy part was about 30 feet below street level. It made for a fantastic view of the ocean from the top of the cliff. There were beachside restaurants on the edge of the cliffs with floor-to-ceiling windows. Noah remembered his dad saying that these restaurants were super fancy and expensive, probably because of their views. They only went there on special occasions, like Noah's birthday. The beach was more crowded than usual that day, perhaps because no one wanted to come yesterday due to the cold weather. Dogs were allowed off-leash on the part of the beach they went to. They headed down the stairs to find a spot in the sand to settle down on.

Even though the water was cold, Mumu loved to put his paws in it and then run back before being hit by a big wave. It was cute to watch, and Noah never tired of it. They also brought a ball and played a little fetch to help Mumu get his exercise. It was exercise for Noah too because Mumu didn't always bring the ball back to him exactly where he was. If Noah overthrew it, Mumu would just lay on the sand and not get it.

Mumu was not an overachiever.

They were at the beach for about 10 minutes when Noah heard a soothing female voice behind him. "Noah Honey, how are you, my Love?"

Noah turned around to see his mother smiling with open arms. The sun was behind her, so her face was slightly darkened from the shadow, but her white smile was piercing through. Her golden-brown hair seemed to glow and dance at the edges as the sunlight sparkled on the strands blowing in the onshore winds.

"Momma, it's so good to see you!"

She squatted down on one knee to his height and grabbed his face with both hands. "Oh, Honey, I missed you. I feel like you have grown so much in two months."

"Maybe," he replied, "How long are you staying?"

"Well, I took a few days off work, so 'til Wednesday."

"Awesome, can you come over for dinner too?"

"Why don't we ask your dad if that's okay first?"

"Okay," he said as he dashed over to his dad.

Mumu stayed with Noah's mom, too tired from all the running on the beach. He gazed at her panting steadily, his tail wagging excitedly. "...and I missed you too, Mumucios," a nickname she liked to call him, as she petted his head behind his ears.

They hung out at the beach for a while, playing frisbee in a triangle formation since there were three of them, listening to their streaming music on their Bluetooth player, and laughing at Mumu chasing after smaller dogs. One time, he got just a little too close to a black Chihuahua, and she did not like him invading her space. She whipped back at him and looked like she would bite his butt until Mumu safely retreated closer to Noah's beach blanket.

"Mom, we brought snacks. Would you like some?"

"Sure, what do you have? Something healthy, I hope."

"Yep, I didn't forget, Mom, we brought cut-up apples, bananas, and potato chips," Noah said as he handed her the bag of fruit. "Here, Mom, you can eat first."

"You are so generous," she said kiddingly, knowing Noah only did that so he could eat the chips first.

Another hour passed, and they decided to head home as Noah had homework to finish before dinner. He asked his dad if they could stop by the sports store to get his cleats, but he promptly remembered they were closed until Monday. He laughed and corrected himself. His dad had agreed to have his mom over for dinner; she also wanted to see where they had moved. Noah was super happy to show her.

While Noah was doing his homework at the kitchen table, his dad started making dinner. His mom offered to help. Noah could see the two of them laughing and talking out of the corner of his eye. It was just like old times, and Noah didn't want it to end. For a brief moment, he hoped her visit meant they were getting back together and could move back in together. They could rebuy their old home, and Noah would have his friends back.

For now, he had to focus on Monday's assignments. Noah liked doing his math homework but didn't like writing essays, especially about books teachers told him to read. He would rather write an essay about a book he picked out to read. He thought about *The Fearless Firefighter* book upstairs and looked forward to reading at least another chapter with his dad.

Noah was about done with his math when his dad set down the meal.

"Yum, yum, yum!" said Noah as he licked his lips.

It was spaghetti and meatballs with a homemade sauce from his grandma. There was also crispy garlic bread that Noah loved to dip in the spaghetti sauce.

His mom made a Caesar salad that she knew Noah would like. She was always making sure he ate his greens.

"Can you show me around the house after dinner, Noah?" His mom asked after passing the garlic bread.

"Sure, but I can't promise my room is clean or smells good," he said, watching his dad shake his head.

"Hmmm," his dad said.

"...and how about we play a board game after? We have an awesome one that will test your brain speed," Noah said as he quickly changed the subject before there was more discussion about his room.

"Okay, that sounds fun, but I do need to leave after that. After all, it is a school night."

They finished dinner and cleaned up the dishes and cookware in the kitchen. Noah grabbed his mom's hand

and took on the house tour. When they got to his room, she walked in, squeezing her nose, and Noah laughed.

"What is that?" pointing to the red book on the nightstand.

"Oh, we got that downtown from this weird bookstore; the story is about some firefighters and their adventures. Dad and I could have sworn we dreamed about it because we both felt we experienced what happened."

"Well, it wouldn't be the first time you and your dad fell asleep reading," she said, smiling. "Is that a children's book? The cover looks so old, and there is no picture on it."

"It was in the children's section. As I said, the bookstore was a little peculiar."

They proceeded downstairs and began to play the brain game. It was a fast-paced game that required you to name three items from a random card query in less than five seconds.

"Name three things that smell bad, go!" Noah's mom said as she read the playing card. His dad flipped the timer.

"My farts, Dad's farts, and Mumu's butt!" responded Noah with two seconds to spare.

They all laughed heartily. Mumu looked up at them like they were calling him to go out and play. They laughed even harder at his misunderstanding.

"Son, you are obsessed with farts, and isn't it supposed to be three separate things?" questioned his dad.

"They are separate, Dad! Would your farts ever be in Mumu's butt?"

Noah's mom smiled and rolled her eyes. "Think it's time for me to go. It's past your bedtime anyways." His mom kissed him and headed to her hotel. She told Noah she would call him after school tomorrow so they could find something fun to do.

After Noah got ready for bed, his dad came in to say goodnight.

"Can we read the next chapter, Dad?"

"Sorry Buddy, it's already late; why don't we see how tomorrow goes?"

"Can we at least check if the story we both remembered matches Chapter 1? I'm not even sure if we finished the chapter."

"Sure, let's take a look."

To both of their surprise, after quickly scanning the words, the story matched precisely what they thought they'd dreamed.

"Well, I guess we did finish the chapter. But if that's the case, then why did it feel so real like we dreamed it, Dad?"

"Maybe we did both; I don't know."

"Dad, it looked like you and Mom were getting along. Do you think you might get back together?" Noah looked his dad right in the eyes with what could only be described as puppy-dog eyes.

Noah's dad said solemnly, "Oh boy, no. I don't think so, but we want to remain friends for your sake, Son."

"Well then, it was an almost perfect day!"

Noah's dad kissed him on the forehead and turned off the bedside lamp. "Sleep well, Son."

CHAPTER
SIX

DANNY BOY

The next day was Monday, and it was time to head back to school for Noah and work for his dad. Surprisingly, Noah beat his dad waking up that morning and was eating his favorite cereal, *Frosted Fruits*. While it sounded healthy, it wasn't, since it was just sugar-coated corn and wheat flour. It only tasted and looked like little fruits, but if that cereal was fruit, then chocolate was vegetables!

Noah's dad entered the kitchen.

"Good morning, Son; sorry for getting up so late." He

had slept through the snooze on his alarm clock three times.

"Why are you so tired?"

His dad sighed. "I decided to work after your mom left, and before I knew it, it was after midnight."

"Dad, you need to let work go sometimes. Besides, don't you always tell me 'Early to bed, early to rise, makes a man healthy, wealthy, and wise?'"

"Glad you are absorbing some of my feeble attempts at parenting, and you are partly right, but sometimes work can throw more homework at you than you can handle in one day. Catch my drift?"

"Sure, Dad, that's why I like those jobs that have a standard shift you have to work, and you are done, no bringing work home with you."

"Like a firefighter?"

"Mmm-hmm," he quickly realized his mouth was full again and didn't want to talk with it full.

"Every job has its pros and cons. At least with my job, it's doubtful my laptop will catch on fire and burn me," his dad said smiling.

Noah went to a small school that was near the beach cliffs. The schoolyard was enclosed by a concrete wall about three feet tall and then a chain-link fence of about

14 feet. It was good protection from the cliff but also allowed incredible ocean views. Sometimes when the fog rolled into the beach, it would stay below the ridge, and it looked like the school was sitting on clouds. Occasionally, one of Noah's classmates who thought they were good at basketball would airball it over the fence to the beach 35 feet below. For this reason, the school did not buy the most expensive basketballs for the yard.

Before school started, the kids always gathered in the schoolyard while waiting for the first bell.

Noah arrived and headed into the corner of the yard. He was new at the school and hadn't yet found anybody to be good friends with. For now, his phone was the closest thing he had to a friend, especially this online game that was so addicting. The game allowed kids to design worlds, and other kids played those courses. You earned more points if you created a course that was harder to finish than your competitors. Kids tracked their points all over the globe. Noah was following a kid in Germany that was playing his new dragon-themed course. Noah's phone typically occupied his time before the first bell rang, but today was different.

"Hey, you're new here, right?"

Noah was facing the ocean at the fence line and turned around with a surprised but curious look. "Oh, I guess... wait, how did you know?"

"Because you weren't here two months ago when school started," said the girl.

Noah chuckled but immediately started sweating from embarrassment. "Duh, sorry, it must be too early for my brain to work."

"That's okay; some people are not morning people." She smiled. "I'm Danielle, but most people call me Dani for short."

"Nice to meet you; I'm Noah." He started to move his hand up for a handshake but then realized maybe only boys did that, so he pretended to straighten his shirt with it instead.

Dani was slender and a little taller than Noah. She had short blonde hair with virtually no styling. She wasn't wearing any makeup or jewelry like many girls in school wore, and her clothes consisted of ripped-up jeans and a long sleeve, button-up black shirt with a collar. He could have easily mistaken her for another boy in the yard if not for her gentle voice.

They started getting to know each other, and the conversation felt natural. Noah was comforted by the fact that she, too, came from a home where her parents split up. It was nice to finally talk to someone else his age about life at home.

"Do you have any brothers or sisters?" Noah asked.

"Unfortunately, yes," she replied.

"Why do you say that? I would love to have a brother or sister."

"You think that now, but what if you got socked in the arm 1000 times over your short life and were forced to wear hand-me-down clothes because your parents were too cheap to buy new ones? You probably would have a different opinion. Actually... scratch that, I like wearing his clothes. It's his sense of style that I hate."

Noah appreciated how Dani nearly hung on every word he said and never took her eyes off his face. They agreed to meet in the same place during lunch.

Lunch took longer to arrive than most days for Noah. He had difficulty concentrating on school when he just wanted to learn more about his new friend. It was the first time in a while that there was more to being in school than just teachers, homework, and tests. He met Dani at the same place.

"So, since you like to read, I have to tell you about this new book I got downtown," said Noah.

"Downtown? Where? I've been there, and all they have are these stores that sell over-priced lamps and tacky home stuff for grown-ups."

"It's the bookstore across the corner from the sports store."

Dani said confidently, "Now, I know why. I'm not really into sports."

"That's okay," said Noah. "Maybe I can take you there this weekend."

Noah started talking about the red book and the firefighter adventures he read about and how weird it was that his dad had dreamed the same dream. As they were chatting, what can only be described as a solar eclipse of a shadow descended upon them. It was the man-child named Kang, or that's what he wanted to be called. Nobody knew his real name, not even the teachers, because he always made sure new teachers were keenly aware of his name before they called attendance. Kang was bigger than most of the kids' parents but had a round, chubby, baby face. If you saw him from behind, you would have thought a college student had lost his way to their school campus. He didn't have a school bag because he never brought his books or lunch. Most of his lunches came from unsuspecting school kids or the cafeteria. Where he got his lunch money was still undetermined, but Dani said she remembered seeing him steal 40 dollars from a teacher's purse once while the teacher was helping a kid to the principal's office.

Kang always smelled of beef jerky; at any time, you could always find jerky sticks poking out of his pants pockets. Dani figured that he ate way too much protein, which was the source of his beastly growth at his age.

"Did Danny Boy find a new boyfriend?" Kang questioned as a small piece of beef jerky flew out of his mouth and bounced on the pavement.

Dani looked at Noah with a distressed look.

Noah looked up. "Hey, I'm Noah; what's up?"

Kang didn't expect the new kid to answer. "Was I talking to you, FNG?"

"FNG?" said Noah.

Kang looked back and forth at his friends behind him and laughed. "Freaking New Guy! You know, I bet Danny Boy here has to use the bathroom after drinking her juice box from lunch; the boys' room is over there. You two can go together."

"How do you know where the boys' room is?" asked Noah. Kang looked confused until Noah added something more. "Don't animals just use the trees?"

Kang's pasty white face got nearly bright red, and he stepped closer to Noah. Just then, the next period bell rang.

"You're funny, FNG, but I am the only kid that gets to be funny in this school. Better watch your back."

Noah looked back at Dani and just smiled.

Noah had no idea where that bravery came from, but five seconds later, he realized he had made a good friend and an evil enemy in one day. He and Dani agreed to meet at the bus stop after the last period.

After school, as Noah approached the bus, he kept looking around him. Dani seemed to understand what he was doing.

"Don't worry," she said, "Kang doesn't take the bus; he lives down the street, so he walks home. By the way, thanks for standing up for me earlier today."

"Yeah, I don't where that courage came from, but I am glad I was able to stand up to that bully."

"Well, Kang likes to go after easy targets, and you're not one of them now. On the other hand, I stopped bringing money to school, so he won't take it, and he doesn't like stealing my healthy lunches. He likes to pick on me because I'm not a typical girl. I can't help who I am."

"No, you can't, and you should be celebrated for your uniqueness not punished." Dani's smile went ear to ear, and she put out her fist for a fist pump. Noah met her fist with his and asked, "Hey, want to study together this afternoon? I could really use some help with Life Sciences."

"That would be cool; let me just call my mom and check with her first."

On the bus ride home, Dani pointed out the unique attractions and history of the small beach town, like the cemetery near the beach that people rarely visit. People would claim they heard their deceased loved ones calling to them when they went there, but most city officials discounted it as the ocean winds howling through the trees and grave monuments. She also mentioned one store downtown was always vacant because they found the owner's baby just sitting in her bassinet one afternoon, but no one ever heard from the mother again. Her car was still parked in front of the store, and all her belongings, purse, keys, and money were behind the checkout counter. It was as if she vanished into thin air because there was no evidence of a crime.

They reached Dani's stop, and she pointed out which house was hers. Her mother had let her stay with Noah after Noah's dad talked to her. The bus arrived at the start of Noah's cul-de-sac, and they only had to walk about 300 feet to his house. As they walked to his house, Tommy, his younger neighbor, ran toward them.

"You guys want to play some cornhole?" Tommy said excitedly, not even asking who Noah's new friend was.

Dani and Noah smiled at each other. Noah knew this was the second time Tommy had asked him and felt slightly obligated.

"Alright, Tommy. By the way, this is Dani, but we only have a half hour; we need to study."

Tommy was so enthused that he didn't even acknowledge the introduction to Dani.

"Come on, come on; I have it all ready to go." He skipped merrily to his front yard.

"What is cornhole?" Dani asked Noah while walking hesitantly to Tommy's yard.

"Pretty straightforward, really. There are two angled boards with a hole in them separated by 27 feet. You use two different colored sets of three bean bags to see who can get it closer to or in the hole in the opposite board." He started to whisper as they got closer to Tommy. "Tommy puts the boards only about 14 feet apart, but who's counting?"

"Here, you're blue." Tommy handed three blue bean bags to Dani. "It's my game, so I go first. I'm red!"

Noah ushered Dani to the opposite board and gave her a few pointers on how to throw the bean bags. Her attention span was great, and she quickly got the hang of it. He had shown Tommy a few things a while back, but the kid couldn't wait to get the bags out of his hands. Noah didn't play, just coached. He had an excellent throwing arm from baseball and didn't want to make either look bad.

He wanted to give Tommy the best chance to win.

"That's what you call a *Drain O*," shouted Tommy as his bean bag toss landed inside the board hole. "And it's worth three points, so I win!"

"Great job, little man!" replied Dani. That's three games to my one win."

Noah liked how nurturing Dani was to Tommy, even though she barely knew him.

After playing for about 25 minutes, they thanked Tommy and walked to Noah's front door. His front door had a cool gadget that didn't require keys to open the door but instead used his fingerprint. Noah was finally able to show someone it since their move.

"Maybe if you stay cool, your fingerprint can be on here one day too."

"Aww gee, you would do that for me?" said Dani.

One of Noah's house rules from this dad was that he could take an hour's break to play video games with a snack, but then he had to start immediately on his homework. Since they already used most of the time playing with Tommy, he decided they should get started studying. Noah was tempted to show Dani and begin reading the firefighter book, but that wouldn't be fair to his dad. He showed Dani to the table and motioned that he would get them some snacks. He grabbed two oranges from the refrigerator, his favorite chips, and two glasses of ice water, and then plopped into the kitchen chair.

CHAPTER
SEVEN

STUDY BUDDY

D ani and Noah opened their Life Science books to their homework assignment. They were learning about photosynthesis, which turned sunlight, water, and carbon dioxide into food and oxygen for plants. Unfortunately, Noah was daydreaming a bit when the teacher reviewed the potential content of this Friday's quiz.

"Wait, what is cellular respiration again?" asked Noah.

"Cellular respiration cannot occur without photosynthesis, and photosynthesis cannot occur without cellular respiration," replied Dani.

"So, they are opposites?"

"Exactly."

"How are we supposed to remember all this stuff? The only easy thing is knowing that chlorophyll reflects green light waves. This is why plants appear green. Everyone knows plants are mostly green."

Dani was showing Noah some sections the teacher pointed out to review when she heard an awful sound coming from Noah's pants. "Pfffft, brap, phew, whoosh!"

"O.M.G., you are so disgusting!" as she jumped out of her chair to put distance between her and Noah.

"What's wrong?" Noah asked as he pulled out his mobile phone and stopped the phone from finishing its second flatulent hymn.

"That was your ringtone? You're gross!"

Noah was laughing so hard that his eyes started to tear up.

"Noah, is that you?" his mom asked.

"Yes, it's me. Sorry, Mom, I'm just entertaining my new friend."

"You still haven't changed that horrible ringtone, have you?"

"Nope!" Noah smiled widely, still giggling.

Noah's mom sighed. "Can I pick you up for dinner around six? We can head downtown."

"Sure, Mom. Would you mind dropping off my new friend, Dani? She lives just a mile away."

"No problem. Are you done with your homework?"

"Getting there, thanks Mom, gotta go, since I'm being rude to my guest."

Noah and Dani worked on their studying for another hour. It was time to take Mumu out for some exercise since he had been cooped up in the house all day while Noah was at school. Mumu was bigger than most dogs, and Malamutes, like Siberian Huskies, were bred to pull sleds. This means they were strong with plenty of stamina. Throwing a ball around the yard was easy for Mumu. When Noah and his dad went to the beach, they would often bring a sand sled with all their beach gear and connect it to Mumu's harness so he could pull it to their spot. Mumu would get excited and wag his tail when they did this because that was what he was bred for.

Noah and Dani began to learn more about each other as the monotony of the ball play led to deeper conversations.

"So, did you get a choice of which parent you live with?" asked Noah.

"Not really; my dad chose my brother. I think because they have similar interests. That leaves me with my mom;

unfortunately, she is less accepting of my boyish appearance and interests."

"That sucks," said Noah as he flung the ball to Mumu.

"I miss my dad's support, but at least he's only a half hour away. I'm fortunate, though. I have gotten to travel quite a bit with my mom."

"Cool, how?"

"She's a traveling nurse."

"I have never heard of that. Was it because of the pandemic? I heard hospitals were overflowing."

"Yep, she converted to one to help hospitals in cities with too many sick people and not enough local nurses. I have no idea how much she makes, but I heard her talking on the phone one-time to one of her friends. She said her monthly income went up 600% because she was taking the traveling opportunities!"

Dani spent a lot of time in hotel rooms while her mom worked long days. Not being in the school classroom wasn't an issue because most teaching went to online learning and endless video calls. They would often be in the same location the next week, so they would stay the weekend to avoid traveling back and forth. This was when Dani explored and saw some unique parts of each city they visited.

Noah was jealous.

He only saw another part of the country when they lived in San Francisco as a family before the divorce. His dad took him on road trips occasionally, but he had only been on a plane a couple of times. He couldn't even remember the last time he was on a plane, and if flying was scary or not. Maybe it was all because he'd been much younger.

Dani loved to take photographs with her smartphone. She sensed Noah's keen interest and started showing him her phone albums organized by city. She seemed much more organized than Noah, and he admired that.

"My favorite album is this one." Dani showed him an album labeled Chicago.

"Those buildings are way taller than any I have ever seen in San Francisco. How is that just a lake?" Noah asked.

Lake Michigan did not look like a lake in the pictures. It extended to the horizon from the beach, making it look more like an ocean.

"That water is fresh too, not salty like an ocean is," Dani pointed out as Noah stared at her phone.

He couldn't get over the "L" transit train suspended above the inner city streets and how loud it was in her videos. He wondered how people who had apartments right next to the tracks got any sleep at night.

Noah's dad got home around 5 p.m. He was carrying a brown bag that appeared to be Belly Busters' takeout, so Noah's eyes lit up. His dad said he forgot Noah was home and only got something for himself.

"What?" Noah exclaimed.

He was only kidding around; his dad smiled and said, "Does chicken pot pie sound good? Sorry, I would have gotten more, but I didn't know you had a friend over."

"This is Dani, Dad. Unfortunately, I won't be able to eat either. Remember? Mom is picking me up later for dinner."

"Oh yeah, well then, more for me," he said, grinning, "...and very nice to meet you, Dani. I'm glad to see Noah hanging out with someone from school."

"One more thing, Dad. Do you mind if I show Dani the red book and read the next chapter without you?"

"No problem, just don't get sucked into it as I did," his dad said humorously.

They made their way up to Noah's room. Immediately, Noah tried to quickly remember if he had left dirty socks and underwear on the floor instead of in his hamper. He pretended to race her upstairs so he could get there first and breathed a sigh of relief when the carpet was bare.

"Welcome to my humble abode," he said, bowing in front of her.

"You're weird, but I like your room; it's a little bigger

than mine, and it's cool to be on the second floor. Our house is ranch style, so only one story." Noah secretly felt better that one thing he had was better than Dani's. "We do have a game room, though," she continued, "that's where I normally hang out."

Noah stopped feeling better after hearing that.

"Here's the book I was talking about." Noah handed her the red book from his nightstand.

"This is weird. Did you find this in a pirate's sunken treasure chest? It looks ancient."

"Very funny; it may look weird, but it gives you the wildest dreams, I swear."

"Did you notice there is no publisher or author mentioned where it normally is? What kind of book just starts right into a story?"

Noah wanted to start reading Chapter 2 and grabbed the book from Dani. "Chapter 2…"

Dani quickly grabbed it back. "Jeez, don't you think I would like to read what happens before Chapter 2 first?"

"Oh yeah, duh, but can you hurry up? My mom is going to pick us up soon."

Dani started reading to herself while Noah tried to organize his room a little better.

"You know it's hard to read fast when I see movement around the room in the corner of my eye."

"Sorry, I'll chill on the bed and play a game silently on my phone," Noah responded.

About 10 minutes later, Dani looked up, "Okay, all done. Are you ready to read Chapter 2?"

"Am I ever!" Noah slid closer to her side of the bed. " Ding-Dong!" the doorbell sounded out.

Noah groaned, a bit annoyed at the interruption. "Oh, perfect! My mom is here now; I mean... I want to hang out with her but ugh!"

"Just bring it to school; we can read it together at lunch."

"Great idea," said Noah.

Noah and his mom went to one of the nicer restaurants on the main downtown street parallel to the beach. Even though they had an Italian dinner the night before at home, it was the restaurant that Noah wanted to try. It had indoor seating with floor-to-ceiling windows to look at the ocean while dining. There was even old Italian music playing faintly in the background. Noah loved that they brought warm bread out right away on the table, and he also got his own personal small porcelain dish of butter.

"Are we celebrating anything? Dad only takes me to these places on special occasions." Noah asked, realizing he was already getting full on the delicious bread, and they hadn't even ordered dinner yet.

"Spending time with my baby is special enough," she

replied. "How are you adjusting to your new school and town?"

"It hasn't been easy, but it's getting better."

"You know, Son, I'm making enough now that I can buy a much bigger house. You could come live with me. There are lots of cool places to go where I live."

Her comment was almost as confusing as the menu, which had what appeared to be hundreds of dinner options. "I think I will have the lasagna."

"Did you hear what I said to you?" Noah's mom was a little hurt by his deflection.

"Mom, seriously? I don't want to move again. Besides, Dad needs me."

He also thought about Dani but didn't want to mention it.

"Okay, we can talk about it another time. Let's just enjoy the view and the food."

The view was terrific, and there were even a few boats on the water. It was dark by then, so the only way you could see them was by their navigation lights. His mom had ordered a glass of red wine with her dinner, and she even let Noah take a sip to try it. That was a highlight of his evening and made him feel like an adult. After sharing a delicious authentic Italian dessert called Tiramisu, they returned home.

After dinner, Noah needed his dad to check some of this homework because he had some questions on math and wanted to make sure he turned in work that he fully understood. It turned out some of the questions needed answering by his teacher as his dad hadn't done this math in probably over three decades.

Before his mom left, they watched one of their favorite game shows, *Left to Dread*. It was about two teams participating in a whacky obstacle course requiring only their right arm. The left arm was tied behind the back or at the contestant's side, making it immobile. It required a lot of teamwork, especially when something in the show required two arms. Noah remembered one season when a disabled woman and her male teammate won easily. The woman had unfortunately lost her arm while serving in the army. She was so experienced using her right arm that everything seemed effortless.

Noah had been happy to see her win, since the first prize was $250,000!

Noah hugged his mom goodbye and headed upstairs to get ready for bed.

His dad came in to say goodnight.

"Your friend Dani seems nice, very polite and friendly."

Noah smiled, "Yeah, I can't believe I just met her today; it feels like I have known her for much longer in a weird way."

"That's how it feels when we connect with new

people," his dad replied. "It's rare to find that connection with others, so be thankful."

"Okay, don't forget it's your turn to read tonight."

"Buddy, it's pretty late and a school night; besides, didn't you read it with Dani earlier?"

"Can you believe she wanted to catch up to where we were and read the first chapter?!" Noah threw up his arms and shook his head but giggled.

"Yeah, Son, the nerve of your friend not wanting to start in the middle of a book! Okay, only one chapter, though, promise?"

"Pinky-swear," Noah promised as they locked pinkies.

EIGHT

CAMPFIRE CARELESSNESS

C hapter 2 started with Zach explaining his first fire call as an interim Fire captain. This call required a battalion. A battalion was a group of fire departments typically needed for much bigger fires, and this fire was one. Zach's fire department was in California. California had some great parks to visit, which meant a lot of camping. If done responsibly, campfires were okay, but occasionally people would leave their campsite with their campfire burning, which a big problem.

It had been an unusually dry winter in California that

year, and the forest was dry. In a dry forest, if the wind blew hard enough, fire embers could spread to other areas and ignite tree brush. That could start a forest fire. That fire can spread rapidly; in this case, it did before someone noticed.

Zach started his 24-hour shift and went to Yuba Forest with his department. His firehouse wasn't near the forest, but this fire had already begun consuming acres of land, so they pulled departments from many state locations. An acre was approximately the size of a football field, just slightly smaller. Noah remembered a statistic he had read online and paused his reading.

"Did you know, Dad, that the average number of acres burned last year in each wildfire was almost 300?"

"Wow, I suppose getting to a fire as fast as possible was extremely important to minimize acre damage."

"These fires get enormous, and what happens to all of the animals, birds, and insects living in that part of the forest?" Noah exclaimed.

"It's unfortunate; I suppose they either die or are displaced. All of this is because of campfire carelessness."

Noah thought about their trip to Yosemite two summers ago. It was a better time back then. His mom would cook burgers and hot dogs over the fire while his dad played the guitar. They would sing along to the songs, which attracted other camping families. It was funny how he would meet other children his age, play games in the forest with them, and never see them again. He made a mental note to try and remember to ask other kids he enjoyed spending time with for their numbers or at least to have their parents exchange info.

Noah started rereading the story.

When Zach and his team reached the forest fire, they could already feel the difference in the air temperature. It seemed to go up about 15 degrees from the forest entrance. There was already another fire department there battling the fire. Firefighters controlled the spread of fire by removing one or more of three ingredients that it needed to burn: heat, oxygen, and fuel. Heat could be removed with water or fire-retardant foam. Fuel was other parts of the forest that could burn quickly. Firefighters must often intentionally clear away parts of the forest that were not on fire, so that the current fire had nothing else to burn. These boundaries firefighters created were called control lines. The goal was to make them around a fire to keep the fire from crossing those lines.

Noah was about four pages into the chapter when he couldn't grab the next page of the book. Perhaps his finger was too dry, or the page was stuck.

He looked at his dad and said, "Thanks for the tip yesterday."

He licked his index finger and slid it across the corner

of the page. The page came up, but so did a faint whisper in each of their ears. "Enciddugo!"

Noah's dad recognized the people around him and realized he was back with the fire department again, and it was just like his previous dream, only now they were in the middle of a forest fire. What just happened? He went to grab the shoulder of one of the firefighters but his phantom hands passed right through. He immediately remembered the feeling he had last time of being useless.

What are the chances that I am dreaming about fire-fighting again with the same people? He was connected to Zach again, like he was his guardian angel. *If an angel can't guard, then what's the point?* he thought.

All he was, was a bystander who could hear, see, and smell everything but not touch anything.

Noah's skin felt weird, like when you come into a warm house after being out in the cold. He immediately felt the heat of the fire, and in front of his face was a cabinet full of fire equipment, including a yellow fire jacket. He realized he was standing on the side of a fire truck. Someone behind him yelled, "Hurry, Zach, get your gear on!"

Noah turned around and realized the person screaming was yelling at him. His stomach immediately felt queasy.

"Where should we start?" asked Jimmy.

Jimmy was the firefighter who had gone in with the retired and recovering captain to find any occupants in the burning building from chapter one. Noah quickly remembered that Zach had been promoted to fire captain in the book, meaning he needed to lead this team. Noah immediately felt anxious because he had never been in charge of people before or of putting out a fire.

"Jimmy, I love your commitment, but give me a second to think," replied Noah.

Zach now had five other firefighters staring at him intently, hanging on his every word.

It was nice to feel needed by so many people, but his body was fighting an innate fear of being a young kid and the adrenaline of being in a position of power.

Seconds later, thoughts came to his mind that he didn't expect. Knowing what to do, like he had been a firefighter for years, he told his crew that they would check in with the first department on site and then probably build a control line.

The team headed to the first department, already working on the fire's south side. It was easy to find the captain as they typically had a red-colored helmet, whereas most of the other firefighters below that rank wore black helmets.

"Captain? I'm Captain Zach; how is it going, and how can we assist?"

"Nice to meet you. I heard what happened to your predecessor, and I'm sorry to hear that, but glad to have you here. I have heard good things about you. I'm Captain Jane."

"We wanted to see if you needed any help but also thought it would be good to get started on a control line ahead of the wind direction."

"The west side of the forest is mainly lined with rock formations that will control the burn; this leaves the east and north sides of the woods. The wind is moving from south to north, so I have placed part of my team on the north side to slow the spread. If you could head about two miles north of their position and create a control line, we could have a boundary the fire will not cross." Captain Jane had a good assessment of the situation.

Noah's dad was taking everything in and felt a bit helpless. In his previous dream, he followed Zach around like a fly buzzing around his head. Hopefully, Zach wasn't distracted by his presence. He wondered why he kept falling asleep so quickly in Noah's bed. Maybe his son was right, and he was taking work too seriously, making him too tired to read one measly book chapter with his son.

Captain Zach's team rushed back to their truck locations. They didn't need all their protective gear to build a control line, but they did need to ensure the truck had all the necessary equipment. You needed to purposely destroy part of the forest to save the entire forest. This included axes, shovels, and even dynamite for areas with too much growth to clear away promptly.

Forest wildfires could spread as quickly as six to ten miles an hour, depending on conditions. Luckily today was not very windy. Zach's team traveled about two miles north and found an area with an existing trail for walking and running. They decided to make that their control line, but they still had work to do to make it usable. The path had leaves and twigs all over it, fueling the fire. In addition, some of the trees on the south side had branches that hung over the trail and touched trees on the north side. Those trees would have to be trimmed or removed so the fire doesn't spread.

"Jack, can you take the smaller truck down the path to see how far it goes before it reaches the west side rock? Depending on how far this trail goes, we might need to call for an additional team." Noah felt zoned in on exactly how to make his team productive.

Where was this coming from? He was a school kid trying to figure out photosynthesis, much less save a 100,000-acre part of the forest.

"Cap, we'll grab the leaf blowers and get all of these twigs and leaves off the path," shouted Jimmy. Noah liked that Jimmy was a team member who didn't need much guidance. He briefly thought about leadership roles in the future for Jimmy.

"Terrific! Ray and I will work the chainsaws on these bigger trees," replied Noah.

The team began clearing away any fuel for the fire. They wanted to preserve the forest as much as possible, so they only tried to cut the branches extending over the path. If the fire doesn't make it to this line, they wanted the trees on the south side to have a chance of growing back. Unfortunately, some trees had to be removed near the ground because their branches were too high to cut.

Twenty minutes into their cleanup, Jack returned to report on how far the path went and if they had enough time to finish the control line independently. Jack jumped out of the truck and hurried over to Noah, almost tripping over himself.

He seemed a bit anxious.

"Jack, you seem flustered; what's up?" Noah calmly spoke so as not to excite his fellow firefighter more.

"I have good news and bad news," he said as he removed his helmet and wiped the sweat from his brow.

"Okay, give it to me," replied Noah.

"The good news is that the path only goes about a mile to the west rock formations. If we get one more team here, then we can have this cleared in about an hour. The bad news is there is a dead Sugar Pine tree with a gnarly thick root system that is literally creating a bridge of roots above ground across our path here. It's a bit sad because I remember seeing photos on social media of kids climbing up these roots and having their parents take pictures, but it has to go. It's a dried-out root system and is the perfect fuel for the fire. I don't think we have the equipment to get rid of it in time."

"I have an idea; take me there. Jimmy, Ray, and the rest of you guys need to keep clearing and moving west on the path. I'll call in another team to assist."

When they arrived at the dead tree, it was a fantastic sight. Somehow, the tree had angled itself south, and its root system grew out of the ground north over the path. You had to climb over it to get to the other side. From afar, it looked like half a dozen giant brown squids frozen in time after a brawl. Noah took a few pictures to preserve the scene in time.

Noah grabbed his two-way radio off his belt and switched to the battalion's channel for this wildfire. He informed the fire department working in the south where they were what his team was doing and asked for additional assistance from one more department. They didn't have enough time to finish the control line independently. He then went to a storage compartment labeled "DAN-GER" on the right side of the fire vehicle. He pulled out a metal box and eight sticks of dynamite. Just holding the explosives in his hand made Noah super nervous. He had never touched anything that was so lethal.

This would have been the coolest story to tell his class at school, after which they would not have believed him and accused him of lying. And maybe he was just dreaming anyway. He had to be. Right?

As far as the blaze went, Noah knew he needed fire to set them off, but he briefly wondered what would happen if it suddenly blew up in his hand.

"Woah! Seriously, I didn't even know that was an option!" exclaimed Jack.

"Yep, desperate times call for desperate measures. Take four of these and duct tape them in pairs on either side of the biggest roots but as close as you can to the center of the path. I will handle these other four and then tie a wicked line to all of them."

~

Noah's dad watched as they quickly assembled the explosives and ran a long wick which gave the firefighters about a 50-foot head start to run away from. He didn't have the firefighter training knowledge or confidence that they were doing it right. His fatherly instinct kicked in, and he desperately wanted to whisper in Zach's ear to make the wick longer, but he also didn't want to distract his son from this dangerous task.

They lit the wick and speedily ran until they were about 200 feet from the roots. Thirty seconds after they turned around there was a large "BOOM!"

It took almost a minute for the smoke to clear, but when it did, there was a gaping hole a truck could drive through in the tree root bridge. Noah and Jack high-fived each other. With his team working on the control line, more firefighters on the way to their location, and the path cleared of the dead root, Noah decided to head south again to see how Captain Jane's department was doing.

CHAPTER
NINE

A WILDFIRE BURRITO

"Captain Jane, who's winning this fight?" Noah yelled out as he walked briskly over the charred black ground towards her.

Every step he took with his boots kicked up gray ash particles around him.

"Isn't it obvious?" Jane replied defeated with exhaustion.

"You probably heard over the radio that at least you will hopefully have a line up north to contain this bad boy. It sounds like company 18 is on its way to assist my guys."

"Yeah, that's good work, Captain. We don't seem to be denting this one, as the wind is pushing it too far ahead of us. My team inside can't seem slow it's progress either. I'm a bit concerned since the crew is very green."

By *green,* she meant most firefighters were new to the department. These rookie firefighters were in their first year of service.

"How about I go check on them and report back? You can finish with your crew here and possibly join us."

Jane's face instantly showed a look of relief. As she spoke, her voice was much calmer than before. "That would be a big help. Thank you!"

Noah jumped in his truck and headed several hundred yards north to their location. Noah saw them fighting the blaze with water from a nearby water tender when he arrived at the team. A water tender was a firefighting apparatus designed to carry large quantities of water to an incident. He first went over to the tender to see how much water was left in case they needed a replacement and then walked over to one of the firefighters.

"Aye, Captain Jane sent me; which of you is the lieutenant?"

The firefighter was fighting the hose a bit as the water came out with such a great force that it was difficult for him to control it. He didn't answer but motioned his head to the right of him. As Noah walked over to the lieutenant, he had a dubious thought. It sure would be nice to have a hose like that when Kang, the bully, was mouthing off next time in the schoolyard. Even for a boy his size, the water pressure from that hose would send him across the playground. He chuckled at the visual in his mind but quickly returned to the situation to address the lieutenant.

"Lieutenant? I'm Captain Zach." He extended his gloved hand for a handshake.

The firefighter turned to him and shook his glove. "I assume Captain Jane sent you?"

"Yep, how are things going?"

"Decent, but I feel like this fire is getting away from us; not sure we should continue fighting here."

"Yeah, that happens... if you don't mind me saying, I think your team is focusing too much on the center of the fire." The fire was indeed starting to spread around them in a half circle. "How about sending a few of your men to the edges with the fire-retardant foam and hitting those bigger untouched trees to slow the spread?"

"I like that. Let me call everyone over."

The lieutenant used his whistle and a swirling arm above his head to signal everyone for a quick meeting. They all dropped what they had in their hands and ran over. What happened next was nearly impossible to fathom.

Noah heard a large, drawn-out, cracking sound coming from two directions. Two giant trees, probably over 100 feet tall each, were beginning to fall. The problem was that each one was falling on opposite sides of the fire. Worse, the trees fell toward the part of the forest that was not on fire. The trees were completely on fire from bottom to top. As they fell, a strong wind from the south came through the fire. They hit the ground with a thunderous thud, causing all the firefighters to jump around.

Within seconds, the trees and wind caught the rest of the forest around them on fire. Even worse, one of the trees fell right in front of the water tender. The fallen tree smashed the attached hose flat, which essentially cut off the water supply to the nozzle being used by the team.

They were trapped with no water!

The four young firefighters instantly looked at Noah for help. Little did they know inside was a teenaged boy named Noah, probably more frightened than they were. Noah started to panic inside. While he had the firefighter training knowledge of Zach, during a panic like this, Noah, the inexperienced boy, took over. His only instinct was to look around for an opening for them, but the smoke was getting extremely thick, making his visibility only about 20 yards ahead.

"Spread out! See if you can find an opening!" It was the only thing Noah could think of to tell them. "Meet back here in two minutes!"

All the firefighters nodded, and a few looked like they were going to be sick to their stomachs. They wouldn't have much time because, besides being trapped, the fire they were fighting was also advancing rapidly toward them. Before long, there would be no open space for them to stand in.

Noah's dad was observing the whole situation. He started to smell the thick smoke and felt terrible for the fire-fighter team, but what could he do to help? He was only a spirit with no physical body. He tried to say something to one of the firefighters, but it was very apparent they could not hear him. Just then, he had a horrible epiphany. This experience was too detailed to be a dream.

What if my mind is really in the story? Where is Noah, who was reading the story?

What if Noah, who was reading the story that night, was now Zach? That would make sense since he some-times noticed Zach's hesitation and confusion. Experi-enced firefighters would not hesitate, even for a second. Despite the intense heat, a chill came over his phantom existence. If Noah were Zach, then he would be petrified right now.

He had to figure out a way to help his son.

He saw them all scatter around the enclosure like deer running from a wolf. It was apparent that the thickening smoke and heat of the fire made it very difficult to probe the forest bed for an opening. The five of them ran back to the centermost part of the unburned forest.

The lieutenant spoke first. "Anything? Did we check the whole perimeter?"

"Nothing, Boss!" replied one of the men.

"Guys, remember your training; it is super important we don't panic in these situations. It can only make things worse," Noah said as confidently as his nerves would allow.

"Call the captain, Captain!" The lieutenant said excitedly to Noah. All the firefighters' faces now felt super warm, similar to when you held an air dryer to your skin for several seconds.

"I will, but we must figure out a way to survive while waiting for a rescue." Unfortunately, none of the firefighters were providing any suggestions.

Noah's dad thought of something from his earlier observation of the firefighters preparing their gear for their trip inside the forest. He decided to see if he could somehow make a connection with Noah, who was in

Zach's body. He got as close to Zach's ear as possible and said, "Use the fire shelters."

Noah turned his head toward the side of the voice and saw nothing; he swiveled his head back to the firefighters and yelled, "Get your fire shelter's out now!"

Fire shelters were part of the equipment in the firefighters' backpacks. They were a portable refuge from fire and excessive smoke made of aluminized cloth bonded to fiberglass. When appropriately deployed, they allowed firefighters to protect themselves from harsh conditions while they waited for help.

Noah called out on the radio, "Anyone! We are stuck on the fire's north side, trees down, no way out, Code Three, Code Three!"

Code 3 on the radio meant life-threatening. The radio was silent for what felt like an hour but was only 30 seconds. The captain on the south end of the forest knew her men were with Zach.

She responded, "Roger that, anyone injured?"

Noah responded "Negative!" The captain told him to hold on for a few minutes while she figured out how to get to them.

"How long will we last in these?" asked one of the rookie firefighters.

"Long enough," Noah confidently answered as he helped everyone get their shelters out.

He then started to look for a suitable location in the middle of the unburned area that was not in danger from falling trees or branches.

"Set up here." Noah pointed to an area near them. "Make sure to lay in them face down. The air closest to the ground is the coolest and least smoky."

The young firefighters started to get into their shelters, stomachs down. Noah went around to each of them to ensure their shelters were closed correctly to give them the best chance of surviving the smoke and heat. When he finished, he looked at the silver shelters around him. It looked like four human aluminum foil-wrapped burritos. He started coughing and realized he was taking in too much smoke. He quickly set up his shelter. Of course, the zipper part kept getting stuck, and he started to sweat even more on his already-soaked face. Finally, the zipper released, and he was safely inside. He prayed his radio would get a response from the captain.

Noah's dad was thrilled that Zach heard him and helped buy the other firefighters some time. He slipped into the fire shelter with Noah because the smoke outside made him feel sick. He wondered how a spirit could feel ill. His primary feeling, though, was a concern for his son. He also wanted to ensure Noah didn't drop his radio outside. He didn't want to spook him by speaking in his ear again, and just as he was about to, Noah grabbed his radio from the side pocket of his jacket.

Noah felt a surge of energy rush through his body as his radio blipped loudly. "Captain, tell me you have something."

"Hold tight; I got you guys. Found you on your GPS trackers. You are in your fire shelters, I hope?" Noah immediately confirmed that they were. "I estimate 5-10 minutes."

"How will we know?" Zach felt blind in the dark shelter and knew that outside the shelter was not much better with the dense dark gray smoke.

"Trust me, you will know!" Captain Jane responded.

TEN

WATERLOGGED

Noah called out to the four other firefighters one name at a time to confirm everyone was still okay. He felt much better after the last name responded. The fire shelter was like an oversized sleeping bag but much less comfortable. The shelter keeps out the smoky air and provides the firefighter some protection from the heat. However, it cannot withstand direct fire. He hoped that the flames would stay away from them. Still, the inside temperature felt warmer, and the air started feeling stale and smokier. He thought about his dad and wondered if he would see him again. Maybe his dad was with him, in spirit, right now inside the shelter.

A moment later, he could hear the faint sound of a helicopter in the distance.

As the sound got louder and louder, he heard a voice over a megaphone. "Exit your shelters now! Clearing a path."

He quickly exited his shelter and yelled as loud as he could to the team. The sound of the fire crackling around them was nearly deafening.

"Let's go, gents. Standby!" the megaphone voice added.

They all moved as quickly as they could to free themselves from their silver burrito wraps. Noah being the first out started assisting others. They began to huddle together.

"Where is Johnny?" asked one of the firefighters. Everyone whipped their heads around and saw one shelter still erected, and steam was coming off it. This meant cooler air on the inside was hitting the hot air on the outside. They quickly ran the few paces over. Noah realized the shelter had not been properly closed and sealed off from the outside. As they opened it, they saw the firefighter inside not moving. Noah surmised he had passed out from smoke inhalation since the shelter was open to the outside air.

"Johnny, Johnny... wake up!" Noah shouted and shook him on the shoulder.

"Come on, Johnny!" yelled another firefighter.

Johnny's eyes opened slowly. Two of them helped him get out of the shelter and put his arms around their shoulders.

"What... khoff, khak, khak... now?" The lieutenant tried to talk, but the thick smoke was causing his throat to burn, scratch, and cough as he spoke.

"Everyone save your breath, breathe shallow, do... do... don't talk," Noah could barely finish his sentence without coughing.

His throat felt like sandpaper, and he couldn't swallow without pain. Breathing through his nose was even worse, as tiny ash particles were swirling around them in the heated wind. The helmets blocked some of it, but inhaling ash was inevitable. He wished they had an oxygen tank to share, but the tanks were back at the truck, blocked off by the fire entrapment.

Ten seconds later, they saw a wall of water come out of the sky, only about 50 yards in front of them. It looked like a giant waterfall that was moving slowly toward them. It was weird that when things were far away, they looked like they were moving slowly but were going quite fast, similar to when you saw a plane crossing the sky.

The waterfall hit the fire in front of them with a massive impact, dousing an area about 10 yards wide. The sudden extinguishment produced a wall of steam almost taller than the forest trees. This was their signal to head towards it and out of the circle of death. They ran as fast as they could, two of them carrying Johnny, until the steam was gone, and all they could see were green trees in front of them.

"Fresh air!" The lieutenant gushed to everyone around him.

"See if you can get to the truck and grab oxygen," Noah instructed. Johnny needed oxygen fast to help with breathing after inhaling a dangerous amount of smoke.

Noah could still hear the helicopter, so he radioed Captain Jane.

"Captain, come in. We are out of danger, thank you!"

"Great to hear; I will send word to the air tanker so they can disengage."

"Most of us are good, but Johnny is sick from too much smoke. Can you have paramedics ready when we get back to your location?"

"Got it; how about some burgers and fries as well? One of the local restaurants donated some meals for our efforts."

"I would settle just for freshwater right now, but that sounds fantastic. I'm sure the team would really appreciate it," Noah said.

As they disconnected from the radio, Noah could hear

the thunderous sound of the air tanker helicopter getting softer and softer as it moved away from their position. He made a mental note to personally thank the pilot because if it wasn't for the great flying, those fire shelters might have doubled as body bags.

As they drove back to the south camp to meet with the rest of Captain Jane's department, the firefighters looked at each other and smiled in solace. The black soot from the fire covered their faces making their white teeth seem to float in the dimly lit cab. Noah's dad was there too, in spirit, wanting to hug his son so badly, but he couldn't without arms. He was so proud of how Noah acted in the face of danger. Adversity changes human behavior, though. Being a kid makes it even harder. Without his quick action and leadership, the young firefighters might still be stuck in the forest with an ensuing catastrophe. He was convinced Zach was Noah. Something about his phantom connection to him told him so, and every jump into the book appeared to make the connection stronger.

Noah broke the silence in the truck and thanked all the men for being so brave. He told them he would say good words about each of them to their captain.

When they arrived at the south camp, Noah could smell meat grilling. It was a welcoming smell compared to the burnt smoke they had been inhaling for the last hour, which had stung their nostrils. A local restaurant owner had driven his food truck to the firefighting location and offered complimentary juicy burgers and fries. It was always nice to see local folks show their appreciation to the men and women trying to save their forest.

"How is my crew doing with the control line in the north?" he asked Captain Jane as he greeted her.

"Company 18 arrived about a half hour after you left. One of your guys sent me a picture of your tree root handiwork. Impressive!"

"Yeah, that was both satisfying and depressing. We didn't want to remove a spectacular phenomenon in nature that had been there for so long, but I have to admit that blowing it up was kind of fun."

"Well, your guys are on their way back, and thanks to them, we should have about 90% containment of the fire. We will just stick around a little longer to ensure the wind doesn't change direction. Grab a well-deserved bite with your crew, and I think you guys can take off."

Noah knew this was a percentage of control, and not indicative of how much of the fire was extinguished, but he was happy to hear the captain's report.

"One more thing, Cap. Your young crew acted very bravely and professionally. Hoping Johnny makes a speedy recovery."

As Noah walked away, the captain yelled, "Oh,

putting you up for the Honor Award, too. Thank you!"

Wow! thought Noah.

He tapped into his Zach-memory and recalled that the award was rare and only given to firefighters who displayed bravery under extreme life-threatening conditions. Noah would never have expected this, and it felt better than anything he had ever accomplished in school.

Noah's dad was beaming with pride for his son. He then started to doubt his realization. Maybe Zach wasn't his son. Just because he and his son had the same dream before, it doesn't mean it happened again to his son. He remembered that he could also whisper to Zach during the last firefighter call at the burning building.

Maybe if I get Zach alone and ask him some questions, I could confirm if he is Noah. Perhaps he was the one I whispered to in the fire truck, Noah's dad thought.

What was going on? Was he dreaming all of this?

It just fits together too nicely. He never remembered dreaming one night and then dreaming another night again while recalling a dream from the past. His head was spinning, and his nose was making him hungry from the smell of the portable grill. Whatever was happening to him, there was also the scent of food torturing him he couldn't consume.

Zach's team arrived at the south camp. As they exited the transport, they eagerly headed toward the food truck.

"Great job out there, team!" Noah gushed as he high-fived each of them, one at a time.

"Thanks, Boss," said Jimmy. " I heard all the commotion on the radio. Glad to hear we didn't have a human barbecue in the middle of the forest; that sounded pretty intense."

Noah emphasized, "It definitely was!"

"Come on, Jimmy," Ray shouted near the food truck. "You're missing our fry eating contest!"

Jimmy shook his head shamefully at Zach. "Sometimes I wonder if Ray even made it past eighth grade."

Noah thought *If his team only knew...* as Jimmy hurried over.

"Whoever fits the most fries in his mouth in 60 seconds is relieved of any cleaning duty at the station tomorrow." Ray excitedly relayed the contest rules. "Captain, can you come over and help count?"

Noah went over begrudgingly and heard, "Jack went already; his count is 23!"

Ray was clearly taking advantage of the free food. Jimmy and Ray waited at the table, each with a mound of crispy, steaming fries on a silver serving tray. The fries were hearty in size, typically called steak fries in some restaurants. This would make them easy to count. The food truck owner was even involved, patiently waiting nearby with a stopwatch.

"Ready, set, go..." the owner yelled.

Each of them started to consume vast quantities of golden-brown potato sticks. At first, they began with one hand, but realizing it was taking too long to reach their mouths, they added another hand. Then, Ray got on his knees, so his mouth was closer to the table holding the fries, and quickly after, Jimmy copied. You could see them forcefully swallowing as many times as possible. Their hasty actions made it appear like it was the first time they had seen food in over a week.

Eventually, the food truck owner called, "Time's up!"

Jimmy looked at his counter. "How many?"

"Uh... I counted 35."

Jimmy looked pleased and immediately glanced to the captain. "How many, Cap?"

"Sorry, Jimmy, I counted 44."

"What? No way!" said Jimmy as he turned his gaze toward Ray. "Wait... doesn't count. It doesn't count because his mouth is still full, since he hasn't swallowed what he grabbed yet."

Everyone stared at Ray as he struggled to finish chewing all the fries, and then he had to swallow before speaking. For Jimmy, the 10 seconds it took felt like an eternity.

"Ahh, but it does count, Jimbo! Do you not remember the rules? I never said how many fries you can swallow in 60 seconds. I said, how many fries can you fit in your mouth?"

Jimmy looked one by one to everyone else around the table for sympathy, probably hoping that they would side with his understanding of the game. All he saw were a bunch of smiles and all he heard was the sound of laughter.

"You suck, Ray!"

"Now, don't be a sore loser, Jimmy," replied Noah, "Alright, everyone, finish your burgers, and let's get back to the station; it's been a long day." He looked over at the truck owner. "Thank you for putting up with my children, but most of all, thanks for the delicious food."

They piled back into the fire truck transport and began driving back to the station. The trip was about a two-hour drive, so Noah had plenty of time to tell the story of his experience with the rookie firefighting crew deep in the forest. They all listened intently and secretly were thankful their assignments were the control line instead of the fire. After they arrived, Noah reminded Jimmy about his fire truck and equipment cleanup duties tomorrow. Jimmy pouted a bit but acknowledged his boss.

A feeling of complete fulfillment came over Noah, and then suddenly, this weird, tingling sensation rippled through the skin on his body.

ELEVEN

THE REVELATION

Noah's alarm went off at about 7 a.m. for school. He moved to turn it off, but his dad was in the way.

"Dad, wake up!" he whispered. His dad woke up with a confused face and turned off the alarm.

"What? Huh? Sorry, Son, I didn't mean to fall asleep in your bed all night. I must have been exhausted. Did we even finish the chapter? I feel like we always pass out before we finish. "

"I don't know, Dad, but if you don't move, then I'm going to be late for school," Noah exclaimed impatiently.

"Breakfast will be ready in ten minutes!" his dad shouted as he headed downstairs.

Noah's dad heard his son crunch through his second piece of crispy bacon while he began to put the cookware in the sink. He wondered if they did finish the second chapter of the red book. While rubbing the soapy suds on the frying pan, his earlier coffee finally got his brain kick-started for the day. As he recalled his dream, he remembered he was a phantom firefighter observing Zach, the firefighter. This experience was just like his last trip as a phantom.

So the big question was, did his son have a similar dream experience?

He then remembered something chilling from his dream. He could whisper to Zach and had a strange feeling it was Noah inside of him. But wait, this was all a dream, right? He immediately dropped the pan in the sink and swiftly moved to the kitchen table.

"Noah, what did you dream about last night?" his dad questioned.

"Well, like the last dream, I dreamt about firefighting again, but it felt much more dangerous this time. This time, I saved even more lives."

As Noah described his experience, the detail was so descriptive and more than anyone dreaming could have recalled. When he finished with "…and I heard someone whispering to me" Noah's dad's jaw dropped.

Noah's explanation was exactly what his dad had observed Zach doing in his own dream last night.

Chills went down Noah's dad's spine. "Son, I need to tell you something but please don't get scared." Noah's dad cautioned. "We're not dreaming." his dad whispered.

He explained how he had followed Zach as some sort of apparition while he rescued the fire captain from the burning building. He also stated how he was there with Noah last night while Noah was helping the firefighters escape the forest fire. He was so proud of how his son handled the stressful and dangerous situation now that he knew he was playing Zach in the story.

Meanwhile, Noah felt a rush of emotions, surprise, pride, confusion, and curiosity.

"How is this happening?" Noah asked.

His dad had no answers as they sat quietly pondering the red book story for several minutes. The time was fleeting, and they would be late for school; they ran upstairs to get *The Fearless Firefighter* book. It took them several seconds to find the book, which had fallen between the bed covers. They immediately paged to Chapter 2.

"Wait," said Noah. "If we start reading it, will we be sucked into the story again?"

They looked at each other with anxious faces.

"Let me read," responded his dad. "It seems like the reader becomes the main character in the story. It's too dangerous; let me take the risk."

"Okay, good point," Noah replied reluctantly, even though he didn't want his dad in a dangerous situation either.

As his dad read through the chapter, they came to a strange realization. The story in the chapter was slightly different than what they both remembered last night. In addition, nothing happened. They were both still sitting on the bed as they finished the chapter. The story they read was about the firefighters getting trapped in the forest, just like they experienced, but instead of surviving unharmed, two were severely burned.

In the book, Zach forced the firefighters to try and escape the burning trees by running toward the fallen trees. In this version, one of the firefighter's legs got stuck, and another had to help him break free. Amid that, the fire leaped up and burned them both before they could safely move. Noah and his dad realized they had changed the story at that moment, and in the version they'd experienced last night, things had changed when the firefighters had used the fire shelters instead to keep everyone safe 'til they could be rescued.

Noah and his dad smiled at each other and realized they had done something heroic.

Neither of them could tell if the book was fiction or

nonfiction. As Dani had pointed out before, the red book didn't even have a publishing company or an author. If they changed the story and it was nonfiction, did that change the lives of the real people from the book living today?

"Okay, now I'm super confused," said Noah's dad. "It just felt like we were reading, not like we were in the story. I am glad our realistic version was better than the chapter version."

"Heck yeah, Zach definitely didn't get an award for that," Noah recounted.

"Regardless, we need to take this book back to *Barton's Books* and get some answers from that store owner."

"Can we do it after school today?"

"No, Son. I have work. Besides, this is your mom's last night in town. You should spend as much time as possible with her."

"Do you think she'll mind if Dani tags along?"

"I doubt it; why don't you call her at lunch and ask? For now, I'm taking this book downstairs. I don't want you reading it anymore. Do you hear me?"

"Yes, Dad." Noah understood his concern, but if they were improving things, wasn't that good?

Mumu started barking because they forgot to let him out to go potty in all the excitement. Noah went down the stairs to open the door for Mumu, put food in the dog bowl, and then ran back upstairs to get dressed. His dad also got ready, but not before reminding Noah to brush his teeth since he had eaten breakfast. Ten minutes later, they jumped in the truck and headed to school.

After getting dropped off at school, he quickly remembered that he hadn't finished his math homework that's due second period. He also couldn't find Danielle in the schoolyard. That was weird.

He started to feel insecure, like maybe she didn't enjoy hanging out with him yesterday and was trying to avoid him. Dani was his only friend, and he didn't want to lose her.

Get a hold of yourself, Noah! He thought to himself. *Stop focusing on the negative.*

His grandma used to tell him this. She always tried to make him more mature and supported Noah's endeavors. He missed her; it had been two years since she passed this last fall.

His first period was P.E. He faked a sprained ankle to get out of playing dodgeball and worked on his math. He knew it wasn't right to do that, but what was more important: getting this math homework turned in on time or smacking kids with balls? Besides, Kang was playing, and Noah knew he might try to aim at him even if they were on the same team.

As he finished his thought, he heard, "BOING!"

He quickly realized that Kang had just hailed a cannonball at this unsuspecting kid on his same team while the teacher wasn't looking. Kang apologized but was insincere, as Noah noticed him snickering as he turned his head away.

He managed to finish his math work in time for the second period. Right before lunch, his class visited the library to gather some research for writing. He decided to use the computers in the library for his research, but he had another motive.

After checking that no one was shoulder surfing him, he clicked on the computer's search engine and typed *Yuba fire, Zach, and Captain Jane*. At first, he got some weird results about Japanese tofu skin used in certain dishes, but then when he added the word *firefighter* to his search, something extraordinary was revealed. He found a news article nearly resembling the red book story he and his dad were reading. It even had the same people's names that were in the book.

So, the book is nonfiction, Noah thought immediately.

The news article described how two firefighters were burned trying to escape. Noah immediately wanted to research how to contact the firefighter, Zach. Maybe he and his dad did change things with their story version.

Lunch time meant it was homework time for Noah. His mom was only in town for one more night, and he knew he would be too tired for homework after visiting with her. He found a place under the shade of a large birch tree to work on his daily assignments. It was surprisingly warm for a late fall day, and there wasn't a cloud in the sky. The unobstructed sunlight made any place without shade in the schoolyard quite toasty. Noah was good at concentrating even while kids ran, talked, and screamed around him. He liked to call it, *getting in the Zone*!

Suddenly, he felt a presence in front of him that felt just a little too close for comfort. He knew who it was without looking up because of the man-sized dirty gym shoes in his peripheral vision.

"FNG trying to impress his new teachers? Dah-hoo ha ha ha!" Kang laughed while turning back to see his friends' reactions.

Noah instantly wondered what Kang would be like if he were alone. He seemed to always have this two-to-three-man entourage around him. It probably was kids purposely laughing at Kang's dumb jests so they wouldn't be the target of his evilness.

"No, I have plans after school, if you must know."

"Is that with your girlfriend, oops... I mean, boyfriend, Danny Boy?"

"Her name is Danielle, or did your puny brain forget that in the last 24 hours?"

"What did you say, squirt? Joey, grab him!"

Kang's so-called buddy, Joey, looked a little shocked to be called upon but instantly realized he better listen to the man-child. He grabbed Noah by his backpack arm strap and lifted him from sitting. Noah had still been wearing his school bag since he used it as a cushion against the hard tree trunk.

"You want to repeat that again, FNG?" Kang insisted while moving closer to Noah, so his big nose was right in front of Noah's face.

Kang was easily about twice the weight of Noah and at least a foot taller.

"Dude, chill! I was just kidding. Can't you find somewhere else to hang around? This schoolyard is pretty big."

"Oh, I get it," Kang said, smiling deviously. "You want to hang around..."

At that moment, Kang grabbed Noah around the armpits and lifted him in the air while hooking his schoolbag's nylon top handle to a trimmed, three-inch thick branch extending not far from the main trunk. Noah was now dangling from it and almost three feet off the ground. Kang roared with laughter and pulled out his phone for a picture.

"Hashtag. Anyone want to hang with Noah?" Kang

quipped.

His entourage started laughing and pointing until suddenly they stopped as the gym teacher and Dani ran to them.

"Get him down this instant!" yelled the gym teacher. All the kids, except Kang, quickly helped the teacher get Noah off the tree. "All of you, no more lunch outside 'til Friday and detention after school for the next three days, starting today. You should all be ashamed of yourselves. Kang, you are coming with me to the principal's office."

"You okay?" Dani asked Noah.

"Yeah, fine, but I really hate that kid. Hope you got a picture, at least for the school yearbook." Noah said, sarcastically.

"That's how you beat these bullies. Don't let them see it bother you. If you don't seem bothered, then they will move on to another target that will get worked up."

"I guess I just have to wait 'til this school gets a new 'new guy,' so I'm not the new guy. Wait, I didn't see you earlier. Were you here?"

"No, I had a dentist appointment this morning; you missed me that much?"

Blushing, Noah replied, "Not really, just curious. Hey, do you want to hang out after school? My mom and I are doing something; it would be fun if you could come."

"Noah, you don't get much time with her. Why don't you spend some 1-on-1 time with her?"

"We did that last night. Besides, she and I can hang out after we drop you back home. Wait... I am never saying the word 'hang' again in public."

Dani laughed at his final declaration.

CHAPTER
TWELVE

SUPES AND PIZZA

N oah waved down his mom from the edge of the school parking lot as they had agreed she would pick him up right after school. Dani was with him, checking her social media feed on her phone. Noah's mom pulled into a spot with her mini-SUV car rental while opening the passenger door window.

"Hey, Honey, does your friend need a ride home?"

"Hi Mom, yes… eventually."

"What does that mean?"

"I know we were supposed to hang out, but could Dani come with, *please*."

"Absolutely. I was thinking we could catch a movie and then grab a bite after," Noah's mom insisted.

Dani spoke up, "I can just go home; my mom probably has a bunch of chores for me to do anyway."

"Nonsense!" replied Noah's mom. "As long as you clear it with your mom, that works for me. Hop in, guys."

As they drove away, Dani checked in with her mom at work. She got the all-clear to spend the afternoon with Noah as long as she was home by 7 p.m. As expected, her mom wanted her to help with a remodeling project she was doing in the kitchen. Dani always wondered why her mom wanted to do these things during the week instead of the weekend, but her mom always responded, *WAWPAW*, which meant ***W**.ork **A**.ll **W**.eek, **P**.lay **A**.ll **W**.eekend*. At least Dani had her weekends to herself, but sometimes that unfortunately meant catching up on homework she couldn't do during her mom's work week.

Noah checked the local movie listings for an afternoon showing. There were only two movie theaters within 30 miles of Primrose Beach, so the pickings were slim. Luckily, there was a superhero movie that Noah was dying to see called *Proximan*. The film was about an alien from an exoplanet that orbits our Sun's closest neighboring star, Proxima Centauri. On its home planet, the alien was quite normal like us, but because of the differences in mass and density between our two stars, it had superpowers when on our planet. His newfound powers led him to a life of crime fighting while he waited for a response from the probe he sent back to his home planet.

Noah started to daydream about what he would do to Kang if he had the same superpowers as Proximan.

"Earth to Noah, did you find a movie?" asked Dani.

"Sorry, yes, *Proximan*. It has good ratings from the reviewers."

"Okay, well, I hope there's a Proxiwoman too. Guys get all the good acting parts."

"It does. The villain is a corporate tycoon. She builds an A.I. army of factory robots that don't sleep, so they commit heinous crimes after their shifts."

"A.I.?"

"Artificial Intelligence, come on, Dani. I thought you were a bookworm?"

"I am, but tech stuff is too geeky for me; I prefer things you can actually touch and feel. Technology happens in a microscopic world that I can't see."

The movie was two and a half hours long. Noah regretted getting the extra-large lemonade which came in a cup almost as big as his popcorn container. He didn't want to miss any part of the movie, so he quietly did a pee-pee dance while sitting in his movie seat. As soon as the movie ended, Noah jumped out of his seat and headed toward the exit. Noah's mom and Dani looked at each other, confused.

"I guess he didn't like it," commented Dani.

"No, this is not the first time this has happened. He's probably in the boys' room, hopefully."

"Why do you say, 'hopefully?'"

"Last time he did this, he was in such a hurry he ran into the girls' restroom accidentally. Usually, you hear screaming from movie theaters showing horror films. That time, it was from the movie theater bathroom," Noah's mom chuckled.

"O.M.G. Noah!" Dani exclaimed just as Noah met them in the theater lobby. "You missed the next movie preview after the credits."

Shoot!" Noah exclaimed. "But when you gotta go, you gotta go."

Dani questioned his response, "Did you use the right bathroom this time?"

"Mom! Really?" Noah replied, "Is it your job to embarrass me in front of my friends?"

"Your loss is my gain," Dani answered for her while giggling.

Noah quickly responded, "Next subject *please*."

They all decided that pizza downtown sounded great. There was a quaint place near the sports store that made you feel like you had stepped into Italy. The tablecloths were checkered red and white, and each table had an old, empty Italian wine bottle converted into a candle holder. The candle would burn and then drip down the bottle sides to harden into wax drippings. Usually, when Noah went there with his dad, he liked to pick at the drippings on the bottle until he was told to stop making a mess.

Today, he decided to act more mature and leave the bottle alone, especially in front of Dani.

Dani whispered to Noah, "Can we check out that weird bookstore after eating? It's near here, right?"

"I don't think that would be a good idea; my dad basically confiscated the book."

"What? Why? I thought he liked when you took the initiative to read."

"Yeah but *shhh*! This book is not normal; I promise I will tell you everything later."

"Okay, kiddos, so are we sharing a pizza?" Noah's mom asked as she looked at Noah and then over to Dani.

"Sure, Mom. Dani, do you like pepperoni and mushrooms?"

Dani squirmed in her chair. "*Eeww!* Can we hold the mushrooms? They're just too slimy tasting to me. It feels like I'm eating frog skin."

"Noted!" said Noah. "No biggie. We can order without. So, did everyone like the movie?" Noah's mom and Dani nodded and that encouraged him to continue. "My favorite part was when Proximan saved the people in the airplane when the humanoid flight attendants started throwing people out of the plane."

"My favorite part was when he reprogrammed their artificial intelligence to start becoming dumber instead of getting smarter. He didn't even need superpowers to do that, just his brain. It was funny when their intelligence was so low that they forgot how to walk with just their legs." Dani was interested in a show's intellectual aspects, which was probably why she was a straight-A student.

"How about you, Mom?" urged Noah.

"I'm not into all that science fiction stuff, but I did feel bad that Proximan lost that girl he liked even after trying to save her."

"Yeah, but they would have made weird-looking babies; it was probably for the best," Noah said as he looked over to Dani to see if he got a laugh from her.

She smiled and politely said, "Please excuse me. I have to use the ladies' room." As she started to walk away, she poked at Noah, "See, that's how you do it!"

Noah and his mom had a good laugh.

When they couldn't fit any more pieces of pizza in their stomachs, they left to take Dani home. It was almost seven, and they didn't want her to get in trouble. As they drove up to her driveway, Dani could see her dad's car was there. She was happy to see the surprise visit and even more pleased that it meant no chores tonight.

"Come meet them," she said to Noah. "My brother,

Donny, is probably here too. He is in high school and likes baseball like you. Maybe you two can practice together someday."

"Okay, but just for a few minutes," Noah agreed. "It's my mom's last night, remember?"

"For sure," replied Dani excitedly. Noah's mom grabbed the leftover pizza box. "Here, Dani, bring this in. Even if they ate already, I'm sure your brother would enjoy it."

"Straight up savage! He never stops eating. I always tell my mom that he is twice as expensive to raise than me because of how much he eats."

On the way home, Noah's mom asked if they wanted to grab some ice cream at the local creamery. She didn't have to ask Noah twice. The big craze with most kids was the frozen yogurt shops (*froyo* for short), where people would pile on all these extra toppings like nuts, candies, or syrups. Maybe Noah was boring, but he just liked real ice cream or, even better, an ice cream shake. His favorite was strawberry and vanilla mixed. He ordered that, and his mom got a one-scoop cone of chocolate mint.

"Was her family nice?"

"Oh, Dani's?" It took Noah a second to respond as he couldn't stop slurping the delicious frozen treat. "Her brother is pretty tall; I think he is two feet higher than me. I wish I were that tall."

"You can certainly get there. Remember, her brother is several years older than you."

"Yeah, but I need to be tall now."

"Why?"

"It would just make life easier."

"Easier, how? Do I need to buy you a step stool for those tall cabinets in the kitchen?" Noah's mom said, smiling.

Noah wasn't even thinking about what she said to muster a smile. "Just with school, not easy being the little guy."

"You are almost the same height as your other classmates; I saw them when I picked you up."

"Not them, but there is one evil one."

"Oh crap! Are you getting bullied, Honey?"

"Don't worry about it. I'm fine."

"Tell me what happened, Son. Have you told your dad?"

"No, I didn't want him to think I was weak. If I tell you, you will want to march down to school, get the principal involved, and everything will get worse. I need to handle it. Besides, the mean kids got punished already because a teacher intervened."

"Well, I'm glad to hear that, but this is not okay. If someone gets violent with you, you must let your dad and me know, okay? I know this is very hard to do in the heat of the situation but try to stay calm when it starts. Fear will make the bully feel like they are succeeding. Be assertive and try to use humor to deflect the situation. Humor also shows the bully that their tactics are not bothering you."

"Okay, Mom, thanks."

"Are you sure there is nothing I can do?"

"You could move back into our house."

Her eyes started to tear up when he said that so Noah quickly changed the subject to anything else.

The rest of the night was spent at Noah's home. They played *Monopoly,* which his mom always seemed to win. He tried to follow her lead, but she seemed better at buying and renting real estate. It probably didn't help that he went to jail three times and had to wait to get out while his mom snatched up all the good properties. It was great spending time together as a family, and Noah wished it could happen every night. He thought about how cruel life could be. Two people fell in love, they had a child together, and then that love was not enough to keep them together. No one wins in a divorce except maybe the lawyer.

As they were saying their goodbyes, they vowed to

communicate more. Despite how great technology was, like allowing them to video call any night, they weren't using it. Their busy lives were getting in the way. Noah and his mom decided that Friday night was a perfect day to video call. They pinky-swore that every Friday night after dinner time, they would connect. They could also connect during the week, but having something on the schedule meant it overruled everything else that could get in the way.

THIRTEEN

FOOLISH FRIDAY

The rest of the week went well for Noah. His dad didn't think reading *The Fearless Fire-fighter* book would be a good idea until they had a chance to visit the bookstore that weekend. He wanted to ask the store owner some questions about the red book. They didn't have much time anyway with his dad's work schedule and a science project Noah had to finish.

He had already started the project but wished he could have teamed up with Dani. She was a lot more book-smart than he was. Besides spending more time with her would have helped him get an A on his project. His project had a solid idea though. He wanted to quantify how many plastic drinking bottles were used yearly worldwide, by region and for each area, as well as what percentage of the bottles were recycled. While the world had gotten much better at sorting recyclables, it didn't always mean they were actually recycled. His research would also show some innovative companies working on plant-based bottles that decomposed in less than a couple of years versus the 100s of years that regular plastic took.

It felt good to be working on something to raise awareness and hope for global waste issues.

"T.G.I.F.!" Noah's dad greeted him as Noah entered the kitchen on Friday morning.

Noah immediately thought *Dad already had a cup of coffee because he was too chipper.* He was too tired to answer but didn't want to be rude.

"Hey, Dad, sorry but I'm still sleepy. Think I need coffee..."

"You know what I've said about that. The later you start, the better. It's just not healthy for growing kids."

"I remember, Dad, it's addictive, weakens my calcium absorption for bone growth, can disrupt my sleeping patterns... etc."

"How about a nice glass of O.J.?" Dad asked as he poured from the carton into Noah's empty glass on the table. "Oh, also I have this avocado toast.

"Okay, that's a fair deal," he replied.

Noah loved avocado toast, especially how his dad made it. Toasted sourdough bread, a spread of fresh avocado, salt, pepper, thinly sliced tomatoes, and an over-easy cooked egg on top. Noah began to scroll through his phone.

"Remember our other house rule? No phones while others are at the table with you."

"Sorry, I was going to show you something I found the other day at school, but I can't find it right now."

"You mean on the internet?"

"Yeah, it's about the red book story."

"I promise we will go to the bookstore this weekend, but please leave it in the utility drawer until then. There is something strange going on with that book."

Did he just accidentally tell me where he hid it? Play cool, Noah thought to himself.

"No problem with that, but I wanted to tell you I think the stories are real." He quickly responded before his Dad realized what he had said.

"Why do you think that?"

"I found an extremely similar story from older newspaper articles in my school library internet archive. Only, in this story, two firefighters were badly burned in the Yuba forest fire. I think we changed history, Dad!"

"Ugh, I think the avocado is going to your head!"

"Dad, I'm serious!"

"All the more reason to focus on other things right now; hopefully, this is just a massive coincidence. We will find out more tomorrow. Finish your breakfast. We're going to be late for school."

They finished getting ready to leave, and as they were about to head to the garage, Mumu started barking uncontrollably. This wasn't normal for him.

Noah's dad asked, "Did you let him out this morning?"

"Of course, Dad."

Noah's dad walked over to Mumu, who was staring intently out the front window. His tail was stiff, and his hair looked on edge. Outside, another dog that appeared to be a German Shepherd was in the middle of their lawn doing his business. Mumu was territorial, and Noah's dad wasn't happy about the trespassing. As his dad went outside to confront the dog's owner, Noah jogged to the kitchen and grabbed the red book from the drawer, quickly placing it between a few books in his book bag. He wanted to show Dani how the book story matched the news article he'd found. He knew he was disobeying his dad, but it wasn't like they would read it out loud. He felt the back of his neck get sweaty with guilt as he ran back to the front room.

~

Usually, on the way to school, Noah would check inside his bag for homework and take a quick final review of his assignments. He didn't check today because he didn't want to risk his dad catching a glimpse of the red book. Instead, he decided to talk about the movie he saw with Dani and his mom a few nights ago. He wanted to make sure his dad saw it when it came out on streaming services before the sequel came out.

As they entered the school driveway, he asked his dad, "Can you drop me off closer to the library today?"

"Sure, I guess, but then you have to walk all the way back to your first-period class."

"It's fine, Dad."

"Why do you have to go to the library this morning?"

Ugh! He had to ask, didn't he? Now I have to lie. This is what happens when you start doing things that make you feel guilty. It just gets worse, and you have to compound sneakiness with lies.

Noah's thoughts frustrated him, but he tried his best to reply slowly. "Yeah, I just have to research one more piece of statistics for my science project. It will only take me about five minutes. I have time before the first bell."

"Have a great day, kid!"

"Thanks, you too, Dad."

∼

Noah quickly got permission from the librarian to use the computers. For some reason, an internet search on his phone could not bring back the results he saw at school about the firefighters. He went to the computer he used the other day and checked the browsing history for that day earlier in the week. He found nothing! Time was running out, and the bell was going to ring soon. He would have to formulate yet another lie to the teacher if he was late.

Just then, he saw an icon on the desktop in the corner that said *News Media Archives. BINGO!* He remembered that was what he used. Many newspapers didn't have their archives on the public internet, but the school paid for this service that collects archives from various newspapers worldwide. Many schools pay for it to aid in research projects. He found the article about the Yuba fire and quickly printed it out.

As he hastily darted out of the library, he forgot to thank the library attendant. He ran down the sidewalk outside, trying to cut around the various students collecting around their classroom doors. He felt like a star football running back as he dodged around students, nearly knocking a few of them down in his haste.

The bell rang, and his stomach dropped while his legs started to burn with exhaustion. He could see the last student, from afar, entering his classroom as he slowed his body down so as not to run into the door. As he entered the classroom, most students were seated already for attendance, and his delayed entrance made everyone look up. They all stared at him mainly because he was sweating profusely at 8:00 a.m.

"Glad you made it," said his teacher. "Did your ride break down halfway to school?"

Some of the kids giggled.

"No, Ma'am." Noah sighed as he settled into his desk chair.

The periods before lunch dragged on slowly. Noah couldn't wait to show Dani what he had discovered about the red book. He didn't have any classes with her before lunch but did manage to see her when he passed her in the hallway. Noah mentioned that he had brought the book and wanted to ensure they were alone when they looked at it. He told her about a secret grassy area behind the school maintenance shed surrounded by tall bushes. He asked her to meet him there at the start of lunch. Unfortunately, one of the loyal followers of Kang had a locker right next to Dani and heard everything. Neither Dani nor Noah noticed he was there because of the commotion of kids scattering around between periods. The bully friend also wore a hoodie covering his head for obscurity.

Noah had brought his lunch today and was very happy

he did. He would sometimes save his lunch for later in the day if the cafeteria had a good selection, so he always went through the food line out of curiosity.

"What deliciousness do you have for us today, Ms. María?"

He knew her by first name because of his frequent trips to the food counter. She was a short Hispanic lady with a colorful bandana wrapped around her head. This protected any hair from falling into the food. Noah swore she wore a different bandana daily, and he enjoyed seeing the variety. She also had a pleasant motherly smile when she looked at him, making him feel cared for, even if it was only 30 seconds a day.

"Sorry, Noah, think you not going to want these... we got tilapia y rice or turkey bean chili." She responded sadly in broken English.

"What is tilapia?"

"Fish, muchacho."

"Oh, no thanks, Ms. María. I'll stick with my lunch. I do like your bandana; see ya."

"Gracías, muchacho."

Noah found Dani sitting beside one of her friends and joined them to eat his egg salad sandwich from home. The best part of the lunch was downing a chocolate milk he picked up from the cafeteria line. For some reason, he couldn't just sip chocolate milk. Once, he started drinking, he finished it. It was addictive, and thankfully, only in a small carton to keep him from overindulging.

Dani made an excuse to leave but winked at Noah. She and Noah went separate ways into different areas of the schoolyard.

As Noah walked inconspicuously to the maintenance shed, he noticed a giant creature out of the corner of his eye. It was Kang!

What? he thought. *Wasn't Kang supposed to be in detention all week?*

He kept his eye on him and his crew to ensure they didn't spot his movements. They were far away, so it put Noah at ease.

"Howdy, Secret Agent Noah," said Dani as he entered the secret spot.

"You can't be too careful, especially because I just saw Kang by the basketball nets."

"Well, his detention was only until today, that was what the teacher said. Don't worry; I was careful coming here too," she said.

It fascinated Noah that Dani remembered so many details, especially a conversation over three days ago.

"So, I went to the library and got this from the archives." He handed her the newspaper article on the Yuba fire. "Read this first."

Dani took the paper and scanned through it.

"Okay, so the firefighters fought a forest fire, and a

few were badly burned. Are you saying this story is also in the red book?"

"Well, yes, but that's not what my dad and I experienced."

"What are you talking about, Noah?"

"Okay, first, you have to promise me not to tell anyone, not even your mom or your best friend; I mean, your other best friend," Noah insisted, smiling, "Can I trust you?"

"Why don't we spit swear on it," she eagerly insisted. "We each spit in our hands and shake on it, like a blood oath but without the blood."

"Danielle, you have to be the most boyish girl I have ever met! Please tell me you are vaccinated."

Dani gushed, "That's the nicest thing anyone could ever say to me, and regarding your other concern, yes!" They gathered saliva in their mouths, spat it into their right hands, and then quickly shook them together for five seconds, saying, "I swear!"

Noah continued. "We first thought we were dreaming about the story because we would wake up next to each other after reading together at bedtime. But then, our dreams were almost the same, except I was acting as Zach, the firefighter, and my dad was this phantom ghost-like creature following Zach. It felt so real, and we could remember almost every detail like it was yesterday, which you know is hard to do if it's a dream."

Dani hung on his every word, thought for a second, and then asked, "How do you know for sure?"

"We don't know 100%, but our stories that are different than the written story are the same. The best part about it is we save the firefighters from getting burned. I think we might have changed history after reading this newspaper clipping."

"Sick!" spat Dani. "So, why didn't I go in the story when I read it at your house the other day?"

"That's the mysterious part; we don't know how we are going into the story. This is why my dad confiscated the book."

Dani started to page through Chapter 2 to see if the story matched the news article. Noah began to sweat, wondering if something would happen. They were so absorbed in the book that they didn't notice Kang, who had been listening from behind the bushes the whole time. He had been told by his friend about the secret meeting place and planned to make a surprise visit.

Now, he wanted the magical book too.

Noah urged, "Please stop looking through it, Dani. I don't want something bad to happen. The experience is very dangerous, just like real firefighting."

"Well, it sounds like you're doing good too. Have you read Chapter 3 yet?"

"No, don't!"

"Chapter 3," Dani said out loud, "As Zach prepared..."

Suddenly, a goosebump chill came over their bodies as they heard the word "Enciddugo!" whispered into their ears.

This time, it didn't just happen to two of them but all three near the book.

FOURTEEN

SCENE OF AN ACCIDENT

Dani's vision shifted from blurry to crystal clear, and she was confused about what she saw next. She was in an elevated passenger seat, racing toward a gas tanker truck on fire on the shoulder of a two-lane highway. The truck cab appeared to have a tree growing out of it. It was clear the impact of hitting the tree had started its fuel tanks on fire. She looked down at her man-size hands and was shocked to see hair on their backs. She also noticed she was wearing pants and a jacket with yellow and grey striping on it.

O.M.G., Noah wasn't lying, she thought. *I am in the book's story.*

Luckily, Noah had felt this experience before; otherwise, he might have freaked out when he realized he was driving a fire engine at about 90 miles per hour. He knew exactly where he was going, and they didn't have much time. He cursed Dani for not listening to him. The strange part was he felt and thought slightly differently than on his last trip as a firefighter. Moments later, he realized Zach was sitting right beside him.

Who the heck am I now? Noah thought. He knew this time he wasn't the phantom either.

Kang started freaking out and tried to grab hold of something but soon realized he had no arms or even hands. He could feel the air flowing forcefully over him like he was on a roller coaster, but this was no amusement ride. All he could see was red metal below, the excruciating sound of sirens, and trees zipping past him. He became anxiously aware that he was traveling on top of a fire truck headed towards another truck with billowing smoke rising.

"Help me, Help me!" he screamed, but his voice could not match the volume of the sirens right behind him.

～

"What's the plan, Boss?" Ray yelled over the sirens to Zach in the front of the cab.

"We don't have much time before those fuel tanks ignite the trailer tank. It will be bad for all of us if that happens. Jimmy, spray the foam retardant on the front of the trailer as soon as we stop to create a barrier between the tank and the fire. Ray, remember using water will just spread the gas fire, pull out the PKP, and spread it all over the fuel tanks. I'll make sure the engine is not miraculously still running," Dani ordered, impressed by her commands.

It was strange how she knew exactly what to say when she had only been a firefighter for two minutes. If only new classes in school were this easy. She even knew PKP was called Purple-K for short and was a potassium bicarbonate-based dry chemical that was effective on gasoline fires. If only her chemistry teacher could see her now. Her mind also felt fuller. She had memories of Zach's 21st birthday party, where he'd drank so much he got sick all over his new girlfriend's white dress. *Girlfriend?* she thought. *I'm not even interested in dating right now. How am I feeling guilty about ruining the clothing of someone that I never met?* It was so confusing but also remarkably intriguing.

Noah quickly realized he was Jimmy after Zach gave him a task. He wondered why he hadn't gone into Zach's body like before, but they had no time to think. They arrived on the scene and quickly exited the firetruck. He promptly strapped his helmet and oxygen mask on. Immediately, he felt better because the smoke had already started to burn his lungs. He opened the fire compartment and pulled hard on the hose to get it near the tanker truck. His anxiety decreased as he was able to cover each square inch of the trailer with foam. It reminded him of when his dad had taken him to Lake Tahoe skiing after a big winter snowstorm. The cars and trucks parked overnight looked identical to the trailer now. Seconds after Jimmy started, Ray covered the gas-induced fire with the PKP.

The acrid smell of the Purple-K was getting to Kang. First, it was the smoke, now the extinguisher.

He yelled, "Hello, can I have a mask, please?"

He was too dumb to realize he had no face to put it on. It didn't matter if he yelled; no one could hear him. He could only watch the action as a third person above Zach's head. He immediately regretted his actions at lunch that day. His mom always told him his actions had consequences, but he never listened. After Zach checked the engine, he returned to the firetruck to ensure the retardant tanks were not running low for his team. As he passed the chrome-plated control panel on the firetruck, Kang saw himself in the shiny metal's reflection. It only scared him more. If he had pants on, they would have been soiled.

Zach was pleased to see his team in action. As the immediate danger dissipated, he began to wonder how the crash had happened. He didn't see a driver in the cab of the crashed truck, so he began to look around the scene.

"Over here!" yelled a police officer. He had been on-scene first after the call came in. Zach and Jimmy ran over to the patrolman.

"Any sign of the driver?" Zach inquired.

"Yep, got him locked in my squad car. He's a little bruised but fine. EMTs are en route."

"Wait... If he's okay, why did you call for an ambulance, and why is he locked in your car?"

"Look over my left shoulder at the valley below. You guys have some rope?"

Dani felt sick as she peered at a valley about 30 feet below the street. A small silver coupe lay there upside down. It was hard to make out the make and model as the coupe appeared severely deformed from the multiple impacts.

The officer continued, "We need to get down there and check for survivors, but I have little hope. This idiot in my car must have fallen asleep at the wheel and hit that car. Guessing based on the tire tracks, they were stopped on the shoulder."

As Zach turned around, Jimmy was already in the fire truck and starting the engine to move it closer. Zach helped him navigate as close to the edge as possible to line up the rescue winch. The winch on the truck had 100 feet of steel rope with a high-speed motor. Jimmy jumped out of the truck and clamped the cord to his body. He got in position with his back to the valley to start repelling down the hill.

Noah had an epiphany as Zach was about to turn on the motor to give the rope slack for Jimmy. "Dani?"

Zach smiled widely and responded, "Noah, you're here, too?"

"I guess so. Most exciting lunch you've ever had, right?"

"...and scary, are you sure you're up to this? I'm scared for you..."

"No time to discuss. Lower me down. If there's any chance for the people down there, we need to act fast."

As Noah moved down the hill, Dani admired his bravery and quick thinking. She helped guide him from large bushes and rocks as he descended. Noah slipped on the gravel and almost face-planted at one point, making her wince. It was good that he wore heavy-duty gloves to break his fall and keep his hands from being torn up by the steel rope.

As Jimmy reached the car, he could hear the sound of the ambulance arriving in the distance. He said a quick prayer he would find survivors. The vehicle had rolled multiple times, and the trunk was compressed to the size of a small suitcase from the brutal impact of the 18-wheeler above. There were no signs of bodies around the vehicle, which was probably a good thing, but then Jimmy saw a feminine arm on the steering wheel as he walked around the car. He peered inside the driver-side window, which only had fragments of glass still attached. Not one window on the entire vehicle was intact. The scene was horrific. Much of the glass was in the driver, and her other arm reached toward the back seat but was now in a position impossible for a human to achieve voluntarily. Her head, eyes closed, turned to the backseat and rested on her chin. Her disfigured arm pointed to an infant car seat still strapped into the middle of the back-seat. Jimmy checked her pulse, and she appeared to not have one, which freaked Noah out even with all his absorbed training and experience in Zach's body.

The car seat had its canopy pulled down, and glass was lying all over the inside roof. Jimmy wondered if the apparent mother had made a last-ditch effort to pull the canopy down to help protect her child. He only hoped the child was still alive. It wasn't easy to reach inside, but he got his most extended middle finger to pull back the canopy. Chills came over his whole body as his eyes connected with a beautiful blue-eyed baby staring right back at him. The baby looked perfect other than hanging upside down, making his golden hair droop like his mom had spiked it with gel. He tried to open both doors, but the car's body was too warped and bent. He couldn't even get his body through either of the window frames as they were now half their standard height.

His radio beeped, and he heard, "Any survivors, Jimmy?"

"Thankfully, yes, and Zach, he can't even tell me how he feels." They were careful not to use their real names in case other firefighters were listening on the radio band.

"Wait. What…?"

"I have a baby here, and I need the Jaws of Life to get him out!"

"Roger that, standby."

Noah saw Dani running back to one of the other firefighter vehicles along the roadside. There were now probably double the number of police vehicles, and of course, the ambulance was waiting on standby. Overhead, he saw a helicopter with the decal "Channel 5 News."

Great, he thought, *the vultures are here.*

Even as a kid, he knew that most news channels were just in it for better television ratings. If they could get a photo or video of something that the public didn't see every day, such as another person's tragedy, they would do anything to capitalize on it. This was one of the reasons Noah and his dad had stopped watching the evening or morning news. His dad would always say, *Let's invite positivity into our lives and keep negativity out of it.*

After Dani made it down to the vehicle with the special equipment, she comforted the baby with a few nursery rhymes she remembered from visiting with her infant cousins. What they were about to do might be a little scary but not nearly as frightening as what he'd just gone through. Dani also brought a blanket that she draped over the baby's mother. It was good that the baby seat was adequately secured and facing backward. The poor kid didn't see what happened to his mother, and they didn't want him to see her injuries when they pulled him out.

The Jaws of Life was a mobile tool that resembled a jackhammer with a claw on the end of it. The claw would start closed and could be jammed into a small crevice. The operator would then turn it on and open the metal claw slowly. It had tremendous motor power and force and could pull metal apart just enough, inch by inch, so the inside of a mangled vehicle could be accessed. When they started working, the baby started crying, probably because of the loud noises made by the metal bending and snapping.

It took about ten minutes, but they finally got the door open far enough to reach in and grab the tear-soaked child. Everyone from the road was watching, and a loud cheer accompanied by clapping was heard as Dani pulled the baby from the wreckage. Dani and Noah looked at each other and smiled. The rescue gave them a great feeling of teamwork and accomplishment. For a moment, they completely forgot they were just kids. This new friendship Noah had, even if sometimes in a weird alternate state of being, was better than any of his friendships back in San Francisco.

As Noah scarfed down a chocolate custard donut that had been brought by one of the patrolmen at the scene, he noticed Dani was deep in thought as she rested on the large chrome bumper of the fire engine.

"Ya know, my dad occasionally stops on the shoulder to take one of his bazillion work calls. Next time he does that, I'm going to tell him what happened here."

"What did you say?" Dani didn't even look up.

"Earth to Dani! Come in, Dani."

"I'm sorry, Noah, but I was just thinking about this whole thing."

"The rescue?"

"No, how we got here. Is there anything weird you guys did when you read the story together, besides just reading out loud? And this is the first time two people came through, beside the phantom, right?"

Kang heard Dani mention the word *phantom* and immediately realized they knew he was there. How did they know, though? He couldn't touch or communicate with them. He tried to zoom around their bodies, screaming and booing as if he thought he was a ghost. Neither Dani nor Noah moved or reacted. He couldn't move too far; every time he moved further than six feet from Zach's body, he felt like he smacked into an invisible brick wall. He felt helpless, and he vowed to hang both from a tree if he ever got out of this.

"Wait a minute," cried Noah.

"You remember something?"

"There is one new thing I learned reading with my dad. You know when a page gets stuck, or you can't grab it—"

Before he could finish, Dani interrupted, "Our spit!!!"

"Huh?"

"This all makes sense now. Our DNA is touching the book, which is pulling us into the story!"

"You licked your finger to turn a page; that's spit. We spit-swore and shook hands. Then, I touched the book with both of our saliva on my hand. Our DNA was combined, so we both got pulled in."

"But everyone has DNA in their skin. Why spit?"

"The book paper can't absorb skin, but it could absorb liquids. If you suddenly had a bloody nose leak on the book, that would probably do it, too."

Kang thought, *I will make sure both of them have bloody noses for bringing me into this.*

"...and whoever is near us must come in as spirits, and thankfully, we were alone today."

"Right!" Dani seemed so delighted that she figured it out. "Now, the only thing we need to figure out is how to get back."

CHAPTER
FIFTEEN

WAKE UP

Noah's dad got a call around 1:30 that afternoon. He was having a hectic day at work and almost ignored it, but out of the corner of his eye, he noticed it was the school.

"Good afternoon, sir. We have not seen Noah since lunchtime and wanted to check with you in case you picked him up early." The assistant vice-principal's voice quivered with anxiety. "There isn't an early release form signed."

"Huh? Um... No, I did not pick him up. Did you try his cell phone?"

"We did, and there was no answer for either of them. Sorry, sir, Danielle is also missing."

"Oh, his friend Dani. Well, they have been spending a lot of time together lately. I would imagine; I mean, I hope they are together. I have an app that tracks my son's phone. Give me a second, and let me check it."

"That would be wonderful, and thank you, sir."

Noah's dad pulled his phone down from his ear and searched for the phone app, FamilyFinder. It took about five seconds to locate the devices connected to it, but when it did, it made a strange discovery.

"Okay, are you sure you checked the school grounds? He is still showing up at school, or at least his phone is still at school."

"Oh, dear! I asked the maintenance guys and hall monitors to check everywhere. Do you mind coming here to help pinpoint his location?"

"No problem. Did you call Dani's mother?"

"Yes, but she didn't pick up. We left her a voicemail to call us back ASAP."

"Thank you." Noah's dad ended the call and wondered if he should let Noah's mom know. He figured he would search the school first and then call her if needed. He didn't want to worry her unnecessarily.

He poked his head into his boss' office and gave her a quick heads up on what was happening. She wished him the best, assuring him everything was fine. She mentioned something about how kids sometimes don't want to be found. While driving to the school, he said a few prayers and did his best to keep his car near the speed limit.

Arriving at the school, he checked in with the office first to ensure they knew he was there. The assistant vice-principal looked worried and was eager to help him search the grounds. The app was pretty good about showing the location but was not exactly precise, probably about within 100 feet of the actual site. It appeared Noah was somewhere on the school grounds. Luckily, most of the kids were still in class 'til 3 p.m., so they had about half an hour before the final bell rang.

The phone app showed Noah inside the maintenance shed, so they opened it up, but all they found were gardening equipment, emergency cones, and building supplies. The shed smelled like fresh-cut grass, which they saw scattered all over the floor. The vice-principal noticed a few cigarette butts and embarrassingly hurried Noah's dad out. She made a mental note to talk to the maintenance guys later.

"Ugh, he or his phone is supposed to be right here," said Noah's dad. "We searched everywhere around this shed except behind it. What is there?"

"Nothing really, just some bushes and our property line."

"Let's check it out anyway."

As they walked to the back, they noticed a break in the bush line that had a worn-down stone and mud trail. They would not be the first people to take it. As they peered through the opening, they saw two childlike figures lying beside each other. It was Dani and Noah. To his dad's surprise, the red book was also there, still in Dani's hands.

"What happened?" asked the vice-principal.

"Not sure... Noah! Dani! wake up!!!" Their bodies showed no response. Noah's dad and the vice-principal looked at each other with troubled faces. He began to shake his son's shoulder. "Noah, this is not funny. Wake up, game's over."

He checked Noah's breathing and blood pressure.

"Check hers, too..." he said.

They both appeared normal.

"I am calling 911!" yelled the vice-principal.

"Wait, I think..." Noah's dad realized he would sound crazy trying to explain that the book story had consumed them temporarily, so he played along.

The paramedics arrived shortly after school let out. Most kids had already been picked up by their parents or the buses, but some remained for extracurricular activities. The teachers were made aware of what was happening and helped keep the children away from that part of the schoolyard, but not before having to answer a bunch of questions from curious classmates. They revealed nothing about who was hurt so as not to incite panic or nasty rumors.

The E.M.T.s checked all of Noah and Dani's vital signs. Nothing was out of the ordinary, and their only reasonable explanation was that both children were in a coma. Of course, Noah's dad knew better but didn't want to try and explain their strange experience with the book. The vice-principal was anxious and questioned how two kids could fall into a coma simultaneously. No one had any answers. The kids were loaded into the ambulance and sent to the hospital for observation. Noah's dad put the red book in Noah's backpack and followed them. The vice-principal finally connected with Dani's mom to give her an update.

No one noticed Kang behind the bushes as the scene cleared of people and vehicles. As he had gone into a comatose state caused by the book, he had fallen back into a small ditch behind the bushes. He was technically not on school property but in a small forest adjacent to the schoolyard.

As Noah's dad followed the ambulance's blinking red and white lights, he got angrier. His son hadn't listened to him and took the red book from their home. He had now caused all of this commotion and wasted people's time, not to mention the medical cost of transporting two kids to the hospital. He hoped Dani's mom had good health insurance for her. He decided to stay at the hospital until they woke from their book journey. At that point, he would immediately relay his desire to return the book and ask that they never discuss it again.

The hospital staff put Noah in one room and Dani in another further down the hallway. On his way to Noah's room, he met a distressed woman and her son as they arrived at the nurses' station.

"You must be Dani's mom," he said gently.

"I-I am. What happened? You were there, right?" Dani's mom sniffled as she struggled to speak.

"I found Noah and Dani by tracking his phone, but they were already in their current state."

"Did they fall? Were they doing drugs? I don't understand how they could go into a coma at the same time."

"It is strange. The doctors are running some tests, but I feel they will be fine by morning. These youngsters play too hard and forget to hydrate properly, so they probably hid in the shade. They just need fluids and rest."

It was the best story Noah's dad could come up with, and he hoped she would buy it. He didn't want to mention anything about the magical book.

"Really? Is that what the doctor thinks, too?"

"Not sure, but I believe I read it can happen somewhere on the internet."

O.M.G. I just met this woman and am lying through my teeth, he thought.

He couldn't wait until it was morning so this could be all over. The kids just needed time to finish their fire-fighting shifts. At least, that's how it had always seemed to work when he was in the story. He patted Dani's mom on the shoulder to comfort her and headed to Noah's room.

After placing Noah's school bag beside his bed, his phone started buzzing.

Oh, great, he thought as he reluctantly connected the call.

"You know, while I was visiting, I asked Noah if he wanted to stay with me. Now I realize he *should*, for his personal safety!" threatened Noah's mom.

"Good evening to you, too," Noah's dad replied. "They will be fine. I am sure of it."

"How do you know that? You were not a doctor last time I checked."

"Okay, I deserve that, but can we just wait until morning and then talk again? I need some sleep and want to be awake when Noah is."

The call ended abruptly. Noah's dad settled into an uncomfortable-looking sofa chair that was missing most of its stuffing in the corner of his son's room. After consuming a giant candy bar he found in a vending machine for his dinner, he dozed off.

The following day came quickly. Dani's mom woke up to the nurse wheeling her computer cart into the room. She felt groggy, and the chair she slept in left her back sorer than ever.

"Good morning. How is she?"

She shook her head. "No change, I'm afraid to report. But her friend is awake."

"What??" She leaped up and moved quickly to Dani's bed. "Baby, wake up? Wake up!"

"Ma'am, that's not going to work when the patient is comatose," cautioned the nurse.

"No, you don't understand. They were just dehydrated..."

"Afraid not, ma'am, but I can tell you there were no drugs in their systems, and her brain function is completely normal. As a matter of fact, the brain scans are showing unusual activity that doesn't match a person in a coma."

"What does it match?"

"Someone that is doing a stimulating activity. Her brain measures like she is active, yet her body lays still here. The doctor was shocked when he heard, too."

Dani's mom ran over to Noah's room where he and his dad were laughing and chatting about something Noah was showing him on his phone.

"What did you do to my daughter?" she scolded Noah, whose face went from happy to scared.

"Hold on a second!" said Noah's dad. "You mean she is still in a coma?"

"Well, I wouldn't be crying and yelling if she wasn't," responded Dani's mom.

Noah whispered to his dad, "The book is not near her. Maybe that's why."

Noah's dad looked at his son like he was a genius and quickly pondered the best way to bring Dani and the book together without trying to explain the book's powers.

"We are very sorry, but we don't know why she is not waking. Would it be okay if we visited with her? My son feels terrible about this."

Dani's mom nodded with an embarrassed look for being so accusatory.

Noah and his dad spent the rest of the morning at Dani's bedside. Noah's school bag was right under her hospital bed. Noah even opened the zipper on the bag so the red book had an unobstructed opening to perform its recovery. Nothing changed in Dani's condition.

What if she's stuck in the book forever? Noah thought. He had finally found a friend who understood him in life, and now he had lost her. At one point, while his dad was using the restroom, so he wouldn't get in trouble, he tried re-reading Chapter 2 out loud again with plenty of saliva on his fingers. Nothing happened. He also started paging through the book, trying to see if he missed something, like maybe the foreword had a clue, but there was no foreword, preface, or book introduction. He looked at the back pages for a glossary, index, appendix, or anything. Sadly, there was nothing. He felt useless and started getting glum.

Noah's dad noticed his son's frustration and started worrying about what might happen if this got out in public. Dani's mom had told him what the nurse had said about Dani. How would they explain that to the authorities or even the press if they heard about this abnormal brain activity thing? He didn't want his son's friend to become a science experiment for the rest of her life.

It was getting late in the afternoon, and Dani's sorrowful mother urged Noah and his father to go home. She would call them if anything changed. When they got home, Noah's dad said he needed to head to his office for a few hours. He had left some work unfinished in his rush to leave his job early to get to school yesterday. Noah sat alone, sulking over his hot chocolate with Mumu at his feet, who seemed to realize that he was not in a playful mood.

He looked at the fireplace mantel with many family photos in various frames. The picture of his great-grandmother, Eleanor, caught his attention. It sparked an idea.

I need to go see the old Wart Woman!

CHAPTER
SIXTEEN

BARTON'S CURSE

Dani was back at the firehouse. Their 24-hour firefighter shifts had ended at 9 p.m., and they were now on a 48-hour day off. That was typically how most work shifts occurred in the firehouse. After saving the baby, another crew extracted the poor mother from the wreckage. The firefighters later got word she would recover fully, which everyone was ecstatic to hear. They assisted the towing company with getting the mangled car back up the hill to be taken away for forensics. Once they were back at the firehouse, they refilled the extinguisher tanks on the fire trucks and then washed and waxed the vehicle exteriors.

Dani realized almost instantaneously Noah was gone when it happened. Jimmy started treating her more like a boss and less like a friend. She knew for sure when they were putting away some of the oxygen tanks, and he didn't respond to her calling him Noah.

Why am I still here? she thought.

She remembered Noah confirming that they seemed to return to the real world after completing a heroic task or their work shift.

This is too weird. Maybe I have another important call to go on tonight.

Impossible, she thought. *Our replacements have already arrived at the station. We're not allowed to work more than a 24-hour shift for our safety and the safety of those we help. A burnt-out, tired firefighter is a risk to the department.*

Maybe something happened in the real world, Dani contemplated.

The red book is clearly magical, and from every book and movie I have ever read or seen, there is an energy link between the enchanted object and its beholder. Maybe, that link has been broken.

Dani decided to have a little fun with her downtime. She entered the garage and sat in the different seats of the fire truck and the fire engine. The fire truck had a 100-

foot ladder on the top with a bucket at the end. She jumped in the bucket and used the controls to lift the ladder to the top of the garage's ceiling. Some firefighters looked at her funny, but she didn't care. She pretended to be doing equipment inspections. She decided to grab a soft drink from the kitchen.

Ray entered the kitchen, clearly in need of a snack. "Go home, Captain. Aren't you tired? Your shift ended almost two hours ago."

Dani whispered, "I wish I could... I wish I could."

Noah biked as fast as he could to downtown Primrose Beach with the book in his backpack. He was super nervous that his dad would come home from work and not find him there. He thought about telling his dad what he was doing, but he probably would have made Noah wait until it fit his adult schedule. Noah was concerned about his one and only friend. What if she was put in a dangerous fire situation she couldn't escape?

If the host body dies while being possessed by a kid, what happens to the kid in real life?

Noah didn't want to think any more about the unknowns. He decided to lock his bike up at the sports store across the street. If his dad did come looking for him, Noah didn't want him to see his bike at the bookstore. He hurried across the street toward Barton's Books. His mind kept going over how he would figure out this problem with the owner.

She's going to think I'm crazy! Then again, what if she knew this and never told us? Is she a good or evil person?

As he approached the store, the green ivy had grown even more; it was as if they didn't want anyone to find the store. He could tell a light was on inside, so he tried the door handle. It wouldn't open.

He knocked on the door several times. "Hello? Hello? Anyone there?"

He tried to remain calm but was anxious to save Dani. His mind started wandering again.

Stop it! Stop thinking negatively!

After what felt like forever, he could hear the clicking and clanking of locks being turned inside the door. The flowery smell of burning incense filled his nose as the door opened.

"Hello, child," the elderly woman greeted him, like she'd been expecting Noah.

"Ma'am, can we talk, please?"

"Certainly, child, we are about to close, but we don't get many visitors anyway. Please come in."

Noah thought, *Well, maybe it's because no one can find your store.* But that wasn't an important detail right now.

"Would you like a spot of tea, Lad?"

She moved so slowly in front of Noah that it made him want to go around her. Instead, he took shorter steps to compensate.

"No, thank you, Ma'am."

He couldn't imagine what the tea might do if the books were dangerous.

As she went behind the counter to fetch her tea, she slowly turned around. "You seem troubled, child. I see you have the book. Did you enjoy it?"

"Enjoy it? Listen, I don't know how to tell you..."

She cut him off mid-sentence. "Child... child... please have some tea."

Noah was now starting to get irritated. First, she cut him off from speaking, and then the light from the room accentuated the large wart on her nose. It seemed to have two more black hairs sticking out of it since the last time they saw her. He wondered if she owned any mirrors.

At least pluck the hairs out, he thought.

"Ma'am, listen, my friend is trapped in this book!"

She started sipping her tea and scowled at the cup. It was as if she didn't hear a word he said. "Oh dear, I forgot honey." As she moved to the cabinet behind her, he was about to repeat himself, "So the curse has consumed you."

"What? What curse?"

"My late husband's. He warned me, but I didn't believe him until it started happening."

"Wait... This has happened before?"

"Child, you are not special. I am sorry to disappoint you."

"We usually come back, but not this time. Only I came back. My poor friend is still in the hospital. Please help."

"Your first mistake, dear, was separating her from the book."

No, my first mistake was getting the book from you, he thought.

"Listen, I don't have a lot of time. My friend's mom is upset and thinks I did this to her daughter. The doctor thinks her condition is strange. At some point, the police will get involved if we don't do something soon."

"Child, there is no need to involve the authorities. Let the book connect with her again, and if she doesn't wake up, whisper the magic word into her ear."

"Whisper what?"

"Endorshiftortus! Make sure no one else can hear it; otherwise, it won't work."

He looked at his phone. He had five missed calls from his dad. "Thank you, I have to go!"

Noah connected with his dad and explained everything. His dad was upset he didn't tell him that he had left the house but was glad Noah might have found a solution.

He agreed to pick up Noah and his bike and drive to the hospital.

When they arrived back at the hospital, they could see three police vehicles near the emergency entrance. To their dismay, Dani's mom was there talking with an older gentleman in a suit, and another officer in full uniform was nearby. Behind him was a white minivan with antennas and a satellite dish on top of it. As they turned into the parking lot, they could see it was the local news crew. This was getting out of control. They had to get to Dani's room quickly. Noah's dad parked near a side entrance, and they ran to the hospital floor. A police officer was standing near her room. Both were sweating head to toe when the officer put his hand out to stop them from entering the room.

"Just a minute, folks. No visitors," the police officer commanded.

Noah thought quickly, making the biggest puppy-dog eyes he could muster. "Umm... I'm her brother. Can I please see her?"

"Alright, but only you for now."

He entered the room as a nurse was charting some information into the computer kiosk.

"Do you mind if I have some privacy?" he asked her. She smiled and nodded as she walked to the hallway. Dani didn't appear to have moved an inch since he last left her. She had good skin color and looked at peace. He pulled the red book out of his school backpack. The book appeared to be glowing red and was warm to the touch. So, he hadn't been seeing things that night when he thought he saw it glowing under his bed. He held it in his arm and whispered the word from the older woman into Dani's ear.

Just then, he heard some commotion in the hallway.

"I have been calling you all evening!" Dani's mom blurted out when she saw Noah's dad near the entrance of her daughter's room.

"I apologize. I had a work emergency."

The suited man was walking behind her and headed toward Noah's dad.

"Did you hear?" she continued. "A boy from their school is missing."

"My name is Detective Nelson. May I ask you a few questions?"

For some strange reason, his strong aftershave briefly brought back memories of Noah's grandfather.

"Sure, how can I help you?" Noah's dad responded.

"I understand the kid missing was in a fight recently with your son."

"I wouldn't call it that. It was a bit one-sided."

"Did your son mention anything about wanting to get back at Kang?"

"Listen, that kid is lucky we didn't press charges," Noah's dad said defensively.

Then, he heard his son call out to him from inside the room, and they all rushed inside.

Dani felt a warm chill come over her skin, and suddenly, she could smell disinfectant. Over a dozen eyes stared back at her as her eyes began to focus.

"Woah! Where am I?" questioned Dani.

"Safe," replied Noah with a smile from ear to ear.

Dani's mom quickly moved to hug her. "How are you feeling? Are you okay? I was so worried."

"Great now. Why am I here? Is this a hospital?"

"Yes, Honey, we found you in the schoolyard behind the maintenance shed. What were you and Noah doing? Your bodies were non-responsive."

Dani rationalized and thought quickly. "Maybe we shouldn't have eaten those wild berries I picked." She didn't want Noah to get in trouble and knew the book was too special to explain.

Noah hesitated but then realized what she was doing. "Yeah, they were good, but then we both started feeling warm, so we went somewhere shady."

"Strange, we found nothing toxic in your bodies," stated the doctor who had rushed in after getting paged.

"Alright, let's get you both home," Noah's dad interrupted. "I think we have seen enough of this hospital for two days." He didn't want them to have to talk to the news crews forming outside.

After being questioned by the detective about Kang's

whereabouts, which was futile, they went their separate ways with their respective parents.

When Zach walked out of the fire station, Kang realized Dani was gone because his phantom self didn't follow but stayed behind in the kitchen instead. For the first time in his short life, he was scared. He had no idea how he would return to his body. He wondered if this was how the kids he picked on felt. He regretted not telling anyone he planned to ambush Noah and Dani. He hoped his friend, who told him their secret meeting spot, would be looking for him. It wouldn't have mattered, though, as his body was nowhere near the red book.

Noah and his dad wasted no time and headed for Barton's books. His dad was very concerned that people were following them, so they went the long route to the downtown beach area and parked inside a concrete parking structure. As they headed to the store, Noah explained what had happened. He talked about the fire call and how they'd worked together to save the infant. His dad wondered why there was no phantom in the story but was glad to understand what put them there in the first place finally.

When they got to the bookstore, the door wouldn't open again. Peering through the stained-glass window, it was dark inside.

Of course, thought Noah's dad. *She's hiding now because she believes she is in trouble.*

Noah noticed a metal box to the right of the door behind some of the green ivy. He could make out the words "Book Return." He showed his dad, who quickly handed over the red book.

"Get rid of it," he insisted. "I'm going to check that we're alone."

Noah opened the metal latch on the box as his dad walked back to the street. To his surprise, a blue-colored book was stuck in the opening. He checked back for his dad and quickly pulled it out. It looked like their red book, only with a title on the spine inscribed with the words "The Potent Police." Someone must have returned it. Noah remembered that the older woman didn't track who had the books. It wouldn't hurt for Noah to look at this one, maybe with Dani, and return it during the week.

He put the red book in the box and slipped the blue book into his school bag just as his dad returned.

Walking back to the car, they passed the sports store.

"How about we get you those new baseball cleats, then maybe a quick bite at Belly Busters?"

"Sounds perfect, Dad. I'm starving. Book travel is exhausting!"

They both laughed as the bell rang on the entry door.

∽

"What were you and Noah really doing?" Dani's mom asked as they pulled up to their driveway.

"Mom, I already said what we were doing."

"No, you didn't. Don't forget I can always tell when you are fibbing."

"Oh yeah, how, Mom?"

"You cross your arms when you're talking. Like when you explained that you and Donny had gone to the library to study last week, and I learned from Mrs. Tomson that you and her daughter snuck in their hot tub."

"Mom, don't make me salty. We did go, but it was closed for repairs; I just left out where we went afterward. Sarr… reeee! Can we talk about it later and make some fudge brownies? I'm hungry."

"Sure, I will start on dinner."

SEVENTEEN

HELPING OR HURTING

The following week was typical for Noah. The blue book he secretly collected from the book return box was in the back of his closet under some old toys he had stopped playing with years ago. He didn't want his dad to find it. Given past events, he also didn't want to read it alone. Dani and her mom were gone for a week. Her mom's traveling nurse job took her internationally, this time to Cabo San Lucas, Mexico. Noah was jealous and yearned to see a new warmer beach, especially one closer to the equator.

Dani had been good about texting Noah pictures

while she was there. One of the pictures was of a crystal-clear blue pool with stone animal water fountains outlined by tall, perfectly trimmed palm trees. The picture also showed her hand with a red and white frozen drink and a fancy-looking straw. Dani had told him her mom let her have the resort's tropical beverages if they were virgin-made. This meant made with everything except the alcohol. Noah couldn't believe the school let Dani do independent study when she traveled with her mom. He considered that she was a straight-A student, and he struggled to maintain a B average. Perhaps good students like that had more freedom, so he vowed to get to her academic level one day.

"How are the new cleats working out?" Noah's dad inquired as he drove Noah to school that Friday morning.

"About as good as the old ones, except my feet don't hurt after."

"Yeah, you must be getting a growth spurt or something. Sorry I couldn't make your game yesterday afternoon. Work has got me sucked into this massive presentation for my boss, due this afternoon."

"Not so sure I want a desk job when I grow up. I kind of like helping people with real-life problems instead of company problems."

"After the red book experience, I tend to agree it's more satisfying, but then again, my life isn't on the line every day."

"It's not every day, and that is what makes it more meaningful, don't you think?"

"Yeah, so did you guys win?"

"Well... Yes. And I forgot to tell you last night, but the coach moved me from the center fielder position to second baseman. I caught the sacrifice fly and threw out the runner trying to make it home."

"Terrific, Son! Nice to know they're seeing your athletic potential, but even better, you are showing it off."

"Thanks, Dad." As they pulled up to the school drop-off, Noah opened his door and looked back. "Can I just call you when I'm ready to be picked up? I'd like to research something at the library after school."

"You got it! Have a good day, Son."

Walking down the school hallways to his locker was more uncomfortable than usual for Noah. Even after a whole week of school, other classmates still eyed him like an alien. Word had gotten out what happened last Friday afternoon.

Lucky Danielle, he thought. *What a perfect time for her mom to take her out of school!*

Seeing a photo of Kang plastered near every class-room was also a bit depressing. It was a bulletin of his disappearance, and if anyone had any details to help the authorities, there was a QR code they could scan with their phone to take them to an anonymous tip website. Kang didn't have any decent school pictures, so the scowl-faced picture made the posters look more like an FBI's Most Wanted bulletin than a missing child bulletin.

"Seriously though, do the adults think we want to be constantly reminded of a missing kid?" Parker commented as he caught up with Noah.

One good thing that came out of last week was it put Noah on the map, so to speak, at school. Everyone knew him and Dani now. Parker had initiated some discussions with Noah during the week and found out they both loved super-hero films, which sealed some sort of friendship alliance.

"You speak the truth." Noah fist-bumped Parker. "Did you finish your book report for Ms. Saunders' class?"

"Finish? Yes. Is it good? Not sure. I had to speed-read the last three chapters last night to finish the report. I don't know why I always procrastinate."

"Probably because you have to do it. It's a lot easier when you want to do something. I wanted to write a report on a different book, but I had to write it on the class-assigned book."

"Yeah, would it be so bad if we picked our book as long as it had something to do with the course topics?"

"That would give kids freedom. Adults don't want us to have that power." Noah smirked.

"Let me know if you want to play some hoops at lunch later, Noah."

The rest of the day dragged, but thankfully it was Friday. Dani was coming home this evening, and they planned to hang out tomorrow. Noah was looking forward to that. The library was open after school for an hour, so Noah headed over there. He returned to the *News Media Archives* and found the articles on Zach again. Somehow, the piece he printed last week had been lost in all the maintenance shed commotion. While searching for articles on the fire department Zach worked for, he found a report on the highway shoulder crash between the truck and the small sedan. His throat immediately got super dry, and he reread the paragraph thrice to ensure he didn't imagine the words.

"Mother and child are miraculously saved from highway ditch crash site!"

O.M.G., Noah thought. *Please tell me this is a mistake. Did our jumping into the book story as inexperienced firefighters cause the mother to die?*

He scanned the article again, and many of the details panned out. The 18-wheeler truck that almost exploded, the driver unharmed, everything seemed the same. He immediately decided to call Dani. This was too important to wait.

"Well, this is a nice surprise. Enjoying the attention at school?"

"I can't tell if people think I am famous or infamous," replied Noah.

"Why is that?"

"Well, everyone enjoys not walking on eggshells since Kang is not around. The nerds seem much more relaxed. They even dance in what can only be described as bad form at lunch. However, everyone knows I fought with Kang last, so people seem to either want to thank me or chastise me for making a kid go missing. They think our being in the hospital has to do with getting rid of Kang. Ugh! I hate conspiracy theorists."

"Yikes. Didn't think it would get that out of control, but I can sense that's not why you are calling."

"Nope, we got bigger problems than fake news about us killing off Kang. I started rereading the articles on Zach and found the highway rescue one."

"Yeah... so...?"

"So, when we left, the mother was dead, and the child was alive. The article from the past says they both survived. I think we screwed up. Maybe we should have rescued the victims in the car before putting out the truck fire. Or maybe..."

"Noah, take a deep breath! Count backward from 10."

"Okay, but what if we changed what happened?"

"When you left Jimmy's body, you missed the update we got at the station later. The mother was making a full recovery. She and her kid will be fine."

"I checked her pulse, and she didn't have one, are you sure? I think I'm going to be sick to my stomach."

"Noah, maybe you checked it wrong. You have only been a firefighter for a few weeks now. You weren't as experienced as the body you possessed. Stop worrying. Go home. We're jumping on a plane in a few hours, and I'll be back tonight. I'll bike to your house in the morning, and maybe we can try and get ahold of this firefighter named Zach to confirm everything. For now, stop worrying without knowing the truth!"

"Okay, Dani, you're a good friend. Thanks for calming me down and for the advice."

Noah printed as many articles as possible about the department where Zach worked. He decided not to read them but put them in a manila folder for tomorrow and then called his dad for a ride home.

The evening was not easy for Noah. He couldn't get the rescues out of his mind. He started to second-guess what happened during their book trips, and now he didn't even have the book to reference anymore because his dad made him return it. Out of sheer boredom from not falling asleep, he grabbed his old cloth face mask used heavily during the pandemic to keep from getting sick and his baseball batting gloves. He put them on and reached for the blue book. He didn't want to risk getting any DNA from his body on the book. He paged through the front and back. Once again, no author, no publisher, no references, only a black type font on creamy white pages. The cover once again looked like it had been around for a hundred years. He put it back in the closet, turned on his side, and prayed 'til he fell asleep.

For some reason, a good night's sleep always made things seem better in the morning. Noah started down the stairs. Mumu was lying at the bottom of the stairs with his head resting on his front paws. His ears perked up hearing Noah, but he didn't acknowledge him. It was almost as if he felt neglected and was pouting about it, yet also ensuring Noah had to touch him to get off the stairs. He could smell vanilla and cinnamon seasoning as he entered the kitchen.

"French toast is served," Noah's dad announced as he dropped a couple of pieces on the empty plate in front of Noah.

"Smells terrific, Dad. Did you make enough for one more?"

"Yes, I would like some too. Dads have to eat too, you know."

Chuckling briefly, Noah said, "No, Dani is coming over this morning."

"Well, if you don't pig out too much and save some for your friend, we will have plenty."

Dani arrived shortly after and was excited to see the freshly cooked breakfast.

"I never get this at home. My mom loves to sleep, especially on Saturdays."

Dani and Noah headed to his room after breakfast and immediately started reading the printed articles from the school library and internet searching. They found a phone number that appeared to be in the correct area code for the firefighter Zach. They decided to call the number together and listen on speakerphone.

"Hello, Fire Chief Zach. How can I help you?"

There was silence on the other end as Dani and Noah's eyes opened wide. Dani quickly muted the call as she whispered, "He made it to fire chief rank, which is the highest-ranking position."

"Excuse me, hello. Anyone there?"

"Yes, excuse me, sir. I was gathering my notes."

"Who is this? You sound familiar."

"My name is Noah, and next to me is Dani. We're

writing a school essay on firefighting and hope you can help us."

"Wait... How did you get my number? I prefer you make an appointment with my assistant."

"If you don't mind, sir, this won't take long, we promise. We have been reviewing newspaper articles on rescues you were involved in back when you'd just made interim captain."

"Ahhh... The good ole' days. Nowadays, it's more meetings, lectures, training, and community service appearances. I rarely get to go on a fire call anymore."

"The forest fire in Yuba Forest, sad to read about the two firefighters that got badly burned."

"That must be the wrong article. I got all of Captain Jane's boys out of there unscathed after the air tanker gave us a way out."

Dani whispered with a thumbs up, "Check!"

Noah continued, "What about the highway crash with the car in the ditch?"

"Son, you are going to have to be more specific. Do you know how often we have rescued cars that went off the highway?"

"Sorry, this one involved a large gasoline tanker that almost exploded as part of the collision."

"Oh, yeah, the mother and baby are both doing well to this day. The mother named her second-born after me, you know?"

"She wasn't injured?"

"No, she was in bad shape back then. Her skin was riddled with broken glass shards, and as she reached back to pull the canopy down on her baby's seat, the car was rolling so badly that it nearly pulled her arm out of her socket. She fainted from the intense pain. Paramedics revived her when they got her in the ambulance."

Noah fist pumped into the air and smiled emphatically at Dani.

Dani interjected, "Well, thank you for your time, sir, and your service. Glad to write about someone with such an accomplished career."

"No problem. Are you sure I don't know you two? You sound familiar to me. I don't have time now but call my office back anytime. Happy to talk more with you youngsters."

Dani and Noah high-fived each other after hanging up with the fire chief. They danced around the room to celebrate. Their worries were unfounded, and they'd changed history with their book trips. As he danced, Noah slipped slightly on one of the articles he had printed that they had not reviewed yet.

The article slid under the bed frame from the momentum. It was titled, "Fire station closed permanently after multiple reports of paranormal behavior in the kitchen."

Feeling much better, Noah decided to show Dani the blue book he had been talking about all week. As they pulled it out of the dark closet, it caught a ray of sunshine, making some material inside the old hardbound cover sparkle a gorgeous shade of royal blue. They jumped on the bed with their backs supported by the headboard.

"Do you think this is a good idea?" cautioned Noah.

"I want to figure out this phantom stuff. If the phantom can whisper advice to the body he follows, maybe he can do more." Dani replied.

"What do you mean?"

"Remember the Proximan movie we watched? The alien didn't get an instruction book on what superpowers he acquired on Earth or how to access them. He had to figure it out during stressful situations, and it took time. I'm wondering if it's the same with the phantom. Maybe the more we book jump, the more we'll figure out the phantom's true purpose."

"Dani, how are you so smart? You just made me remember something from my trip inside the burning forest. The rookie team left their oxygen tanks by the water tanker. They couldn't grab them after the flaming trees fell. A couple of times, when I was surrounded by thick, black smoke, I could breathe perfectly fine. All the other firefighters were choking and gagging. I wondered how I had a pocket of fresh air around me, and now I think it was the phantom. He must have been absorbing the smoke around me. Too bad my dad didn't even realize it."

PLEASE LEAVE A REVIEW AND/OR A RATING

If you enjoyed this book, it would be tremendously helpful to me if you were able to leave a review or, at the very least, a star rating on Amazon or wherever you picked up this book. **Star Ratings and Reviews help me gain visibility**, and they can bring my books to the attention of other interested readers. Thank you!

To leave a review/rating on Amazon, click the link below for e-books or scan the QR code if this is a print version.

E-book
https://amzn.to/49vMrQO

Printed Versions

A Message from J.W. Jarvis

Building a relationship with my readers is the very best thing about writing. **Join my VIP Reader Club** for exclusive information on new books, discounts, plus obtain the **Fire Incident Report** from the building fire where Noah saved the captain. You will find out the name of the fire department, the cause of the fire, where it started, how much damage it did, and much more!

Just visit
https://downloads.authorjwjarvis.com/firereport
or scan the QR code below with your phone

ABOUT THE AUTHOR

J.W. Jarvis lives in sunny California but is originally from the suburbs of the Windy City. When he's not thinking of ways to create inspiring characters for young minds, you can find him reading, golfing, traveling, or just sipping a hot vanilla latte. Visit J.W. Jarvis at www.authorjwjarvis.com

facebook.com/authorjwjarvis

x.com/authorjwjarvis

instagram.com/authorjwjarvis